CHARMS AND THE CURSED COVEN

A WILLIAMS WITCH MYSTERY

BOOK NINE

ELOISE EVERHART

ALORIUM PUBLISHING

PB ISBN: 978-1-962759-08-3

Author: Eloise Everhart

Editors: Rashida Breen and Amanda Kruse

Cover design by GetCovers

CHAPTER 1

I slammed the kettle onto the stovetop and turned on the burner. I hunched over it, my fingers digging into the oven door handle. My attention was focused on the dining room table to the left of me, specifically on the woman sitting at it as if it were the most normal thing in the world for her to be seated in my kitchen between my daughter, Grace, and my fiancé, Chris. It had been almost twenty years since I'd seen my mother, twenty years since she had taken off in the middle of the day, abandoning my infant daughter in her crib for hours until I got home from work. I ground my teeth. At the time, I had been terrified something had happened to my mother. But after I went so long with no word, after she ignored all my attempts to contact her, she just showed up out of the blue. At the sight of her, all I had left inside was fury.

"Dani, do you need any help in there?" Lori asked, her voice calm.

I flinched as the kettle screeched. I turned off the heat and flipped up the steam whistle. "I've got it."

"Are you—" Lori began.

"I said I've got it." I grabbed mugs from the cupboard and

banged them down on the counter. "Chamomile or tension tamer?"

Grace cleared her throat. "Tension tamer sounds great."

I tossed tea bags into the cups, filled them with water, then carted them, one by one, to the table. The movement of crossing back and forth, depositing mug after mug in front of Grace, Lori, and Chris helped calm my nerves. By the time I set my mug down, my fury had cooled to a simmering rage. I breathed in through my nose and out through my mouth as I took a seat between Grace and Chris, opposite my mother. I had never been so angry before. Lori was here for a reason.

Her words replayed in my head. *I stayed away as long as I could. The darkness is coming faster than I predicted. And now we're running out of time.* The only emotion stronger than the anger was the curiosity that statement fueled. *What darkness? How are we running out of time to break the curse?*

I glanced between Lori, Grace, and Chris, my eyes lingering on the bruise on his forehead from where Justin had bashed him over the head with a glass globe, and cleared my throat. "Why are you here, Mother?"

Lori gave me a weak smile and cocked her head toward Chris. "This is a private conversation. Between family."

"No," I said.

Lori opened her mouth, and I shook my head.

"Chris is my partner. He knows everything. He isn't going anywhere. Whatever it is you came to tell me, you can say it in front of him. Then you can leave."

Lori winced and fidgeted in her seat. "I'm not sure where to begin."

I glowered at her. "Why don't you start—"

Lori squealed with delight and bent over, reaching toward my familiar, Charlie, who had just sauntered into the room. He had just hit a year old, and he was a big cat. He weighed almost twenty-five pounds and came up to just below my knees. It was one of the benefits of being a witch familiar. They lived longer and grew bigger than their normal counterparts. He wasn't done growing yet. I suspected he would end up past my knees and over thirty pounds by the time he was done. I sincerely hoped he would stop wanting to be carted around in my purse when he got that big. Charlie strutted across the room, his tail high behind him, and sniffed at Lori's fingertips. He ducked his head under her waiting hand and purred.

"What's his name?" Lori looked up at me as Charlie turned and twisted his way through Grace's legs to stop at my feet.

"Charlie." I scooped him up and held him close to my chest, kissing the top of his head. "Traitor," I murmured in his ear.

"Let's get back on track. You returned to the great state of Washington for a reason. What did you come here to say?" Grace asked.

Lori chewed on her lip, her eyes darting between everyone at the table. Her shoulders slumped. "I should have practiced a speech or something. I'm not good at this. You know, talking to people. How about you ask me questions, and I'll do my best to answer them?"

My jaw clenched, and I pulled Charlie closer to my chest. He tucked his head under my ear and purred until my shoulders lowered. I closed my eyes, turned my head away, and asked one of the questions that had been on my mind since she'd disappeared. "Where have you been?"

"Traveling. I had things to figure out."

I snorted. "And you couldn't return a phone call?"

"I… it was complicated."

Charlie massaged my shoulder with his giant paws and pushed his head farther against mine. He purred directly into my ear. I exhaled, releasing a bit more tension. "Okay. That's wonderfully vague. What have you been working on?"

"The curse."

My eyes flicked open, and I stared at Lori.

She clasped her mug in front of her with her head bowed over it. Her dark-brown hair, streaked with white, hung over her face, concealing it from view. "It needs to be broken. I know how. But I had to get it all in the correct order so we know what to do. It's hard when the visions come in out of sync."

I opened my mouth and closed it again. Grace, Lori, and I were all witches with powers of divination. It was part of being a witch of the Williams line. Grace was particularly skilled at looking into the past with her powers. She picked up emotional resonance left behind on objects much better than I could. But on the flip side, I could track people with magic much faster and more efficiently than Grace, and my handle on using divination to understand the here and now was stronger. I chewed my lip. I had never given much thought to what my mother's specialty was. She made it sound like she was much more future focused.

"Have you figured out the order?" Grace asked.

I blinked and refocused on Lori's face as she set a notebook down in front of her. It was almost identical to the ones my grandmother had left me. Through them, I had learned almost everything I knew about how magic worked. For the past year, they had been delivered by some unknown benefactor whenever I was ready, or in need, to learn something new. Bile rose in my throat as I realized who had been delivering them. I narrowed my eyes. My grandmother had trusted my mother with the notebooks. *Why didn't Gran leave them with Betty? She was already looking after me. Why would my gran give my mother a way into my life again?*

Lori tapped the book with her fingers. "I wrote it all down in here."

The words were out of my mouth before I could stop them. "Then leave the notebook and go. It's what you're good at."

I inwardly winced as Lori flinched. "If only it were that easy. We all have to be there to break the curse. It won't work if any of us are missing."

I sagged in my seat. "Of course we do."

Grace put one gloved hand over Lori's and another on my shoulder. She squeezed, comforting me. Having my mother present, after all this time, was throwing me for an emotional loop. My anger was quickly fading as my childhood despair over not being good enough reared its ugly head. Chris slipped his hand under the table and put it on my knee. Between Grace, Chris, and Charlie, I recentered myself.

I exhaled slowly and shook my head to clear it. My mother was here for a reason, and focusing on my hurt feelings wouldn't do me any good. The curse wasn't going to break itself. And this family desperately needed it broken. While it had hit me the lightest out of me and Grace, it was still untenable at times. I could never shut off the visions. I could never stop feeling what others felt when I touched stuff. Grace had it worse with nightmares, emotional feedback loops, where what she picked up from others played over and over, getting more and more intense with each iteration until she was a sobbing mess on the floor. She had to maintain a barrier between her and the rest of the world at all times, but she couldn't live in gloves and long-sleeved shirts forever. If my mother knew how to break this curse, then we had to do it.

I straightened in my chair and focused on the next question. "How do you know now is the right time?"

"I don't." Lori sighed. "All I know is that the darkness is coming, and we won't have a chance at breaking it again if we don't do something now. It's not that now is the right time. It's that now is the only time we have left."

"What is the darkness?" I asked. "And how do you know it's coming now if everything comes to you out of order?"

"I—"

The house shook violently under us, cutting off Lori's words. Grace's mug fell to the floor, crashing across the hardwood. Loud thumps sounded above our heads as things fell off shelves around the house. I clutched Charlie to my chest. While occasional earthquakes occurred near Seattle, I had never felt something so powerful since moving out to live on Whidbey Island. My heart skipped a beat as the entire room was bathed in a bright-green light.

I stumbled to my feet as the shaking stopped and surged toward the front door, the others close on my heels. I slid to a stop on my front porch, Charlie still clutched to my chest, and stared. My jaw dropped. Trees had fallen over. And in the distance, in the heart of Point Pleasant, was a pillar of green flame.

"Oh no! It's too late." Lori stepped up next to me. "It's already here."

CHAPTER 2

Chris had his hand on my knee as I drove. I gripped the steering wheel so tightly my fingers ached. The only thing tethering me to that moment, that prevented me from spiraling into terror, was his hand. I tried not to follow my panicked thoughts too closely. They bounced from memories of my recent confrontation with just a fragment of the Outsider to worries about what my mother could have meant when she said we were running out of time to break the curse. If she was right, we might have missed our opportunity. No matter how much I focused on the road ahead, I couldn't ignore the dread pooling in my gut.

I glanced in the rear-view mirror. Grace sat stiffly in her seat, her gloved hands hugging Charlie to her chest. Lori sat beside her, staring blankly out the window, her eyes strangely unfocused. Even with her impassive face, I could sense the anxiety rolling off her in waves. The cloying emotion filled my lungs, making it hard to breathe. My eyes flicked between the road and Grace's reflection. If Lori's anxiety was strong enough for me to feel, it must have been almost unbearable for Grace. She was so much better at picking up emotions than I was. Unfortunately, she couldn't turn it off. Neither of us could.

My breath caught in my throat as I turned onto the road leading up to Meredith Walker's house. I tensed, my arms beginning to shake. The green flames had died down as we drove, but the glow of it seeped from a giant crack that ran down the length of the roadway, pushing up the asphalt in a jagged line on either side. I slowed the car and parked twenty feet away from the end of the crack. My legs shook under me as I stepped out of the car, my head craning back so I could take in the devastation.

Meredith's house was mostly rubble. I stumbled toward what was left of it. The front half had collapsed. I could see straight into the dining room. The living room was just gone. On either side of the house, the neighboring properties sagged, their siding warped from heat.

"Has she escaped?" Chris asked.

My head jerked toward him, my mouth opening and closing. I didn't know. This looked like something had burst out of the building's very foundation. Meredith's ghost had been locked away inside the home, under layers and layers of wards. But this... this looked like a prison break.

Grace moved in front of me, blocking my view. Her brows furrowed, and panic danced behind her eyes. "What are we going to do?"

I swallowed and focused my mind on the task at hand. "This looks bad, but we can't make any assumptions. Let's check the wards to see if they've broken. And if they have, search the area for signs of how. This shouldn't be possible."

The Wardens of the West had assured me that the wards in place were strong enough to hold her. They were built using Warden secrets, and they'd claimed only Wardens could break them.

I gritted my teeth and inched toward the house. I had a feeling they had been overly confident when they'd made that promise. "Let's spread out, but stay in each other's lines of sight. Be careful. Don't touch anything. I'll loop to the left. Grace and Lori, go right."

"I'll call for backup. We need these roads blocked ASAP." Chris pulled out his phone and stepped to the side.

I squared my shoulders and willed my hands to stop shaking as I edged my way around the broken asphalt and toward the house. I tuned out Chris's voice as I eyed the green glow being emitted from the cracks in the roadway. *Is it safe to cross it? What if this is a trap? Could I get stuck on the other side?*

I stared at it, debating the best way forward, when a red work truck screeched to a halt forty feet from me. I tensed as the door flew open but relaxed as Megan, a member of my coven, launched herself out of the driver's seat.

Megan barreled toward me and pulled me into a hug. "Is anyone hurt?"

"We just got here." I squeezed her back. It was hard to imagine that not too long ago, I hadn't trusted her. I had been a victim of her curse, which made everyone inherently distrust her. Luckily, a spell let me see her as she really was, and over the past few months, she had become a rock in my life. She was one of my best friends, next to Heather.

Megan pulled back and studied my face before glancing over her shoulder at the truck. I peered behind her as Izzy slipped out of the passenger seat. Izzy was a local reporter who had recently discovered that she was a witch as well. She could see and talk to ghosts, which had thrown her into the deep end quickly. Ghosts almost always wanted justice, and they'd hounded her for it. She stared slack-jawed at Meredith's house.

"Why did you—" I began.

Megan's eyes widened, and she stepped around me. "Lori?"

"Hi, Meg," Lori said. "I'm glad to see you've made some friends."

My hackles rose at the sound of my mother's voice. I knew Megan and Lori had met before and that Lori had helped create the spell to mitigate the effects of Megan's curse, but it didn't make the situation any less off-putting. Megan was *my* friend.

I ground my teeth and turned. "We're in a coven together."

"That's wonderful." Lori floated toward her on graceful feet. She had always moved like a dancer. She cocked her head toward Megan's truck. "Who's that?"

"A new witch. I was taking her back to my place when we saw the fire, and I didn't want to waste time dropping her off. Plus, if *this*"—Megan gestured toward the half-collapsed house across the street from us—"is as big as I think it is, every witch in town needs to know about it."

"What type of witch?" Lori asked.

I cleared my throat. "If this is as important as it looks, then we need to be quick about this. We can catch up later."

"All right." Lori shrugged and meandered back toward Grace.

Megan stepped in front of me and lowered her voice. "Dani. Be nice. She's come all this way—"

"That woman doesn't deserve nice." I spun and stalked toward the truck. "I'll show Izzy how to look for hidden magic. Let's regroup in five."

Megan scoffed but didn't argue. While we had never discussed Lori, it was no secret that she had been a bad mother. Megan wouldn't push me on my behavior. At least, not yet.

I came to a stop in front of Izzy, who had her arms wrapped around her stomach. Her muted-teal hair was pulled back into a loose ponytail. Her strawberry-blond roots looked less stark under the green light. "Are you ready for a witch lesson?" I asked.

Izzy wet her lips and nodded.

"You can almost always see magic when someone is casting a spell," I began.

"Like your golden light?"

I nodded. "And your blue water. It's not physically there, but if you're a witch, you can see it. And some spells linger. It can be like a residue or an enchantment placed on an object or place. To see it, you have to specifically look for it. I find it's easiest if I unfocus my eyes. You're not trying to see what's here visibly. You're trying to see beyond it. Once you've done that, pull your magic to the surface. Not to cast a spell but to feel it. Then... then will yourself to see what's hidden. Got it?"

"I'll try."

I shook out my arms, relaxed my gaze, willed my magic to the surface, and looked at the property again. It was almost like looking at a stereogram. Relaxing my gaze while running my magic through my system caused hidden images to pop out. The green flames flared to life. With my eyes relaxed, the flames were almost two stories tall. I squinted past them and studied the ground. The last time I had checked on the property, there had been red chains of symbols worked into the very soil around the house. They'd flowed through the foundation, sinking into the wood. Those chains were broken, the red seeping into the ground like spilled milk. My knees buckled under me. Not a single chain remained in place.

I was so focused on my fear that I almost missed it when a second startled sensation passed through me. I only noticed it because the startled sensation wasn't afraid like my own, and the lack of fear pulled my focus. The emotion came from Charlie. My head jerked in his direction. He was inside Meredith's house.

"What are you doing in there?" I murmured.

I scanned the ground, checking for signs of a hidden trap spell, but found nothing. The green flames were built-up magic escaping into the air. No active effects lingered in sight. I tentatively reached forward. Nothing happened as the tips of my fingers dipped into the fire. Holding my breath, I darted through it to the other side. The hairs on my arms briefly stood on end but settled as soon as I crossed to the other side. I closed my eyes, checking on myself internally. Stepping through it had scared me, but I felt no lasting effect.

As I opened my eyes, Charlie poked his head out from inside the house and chirped at me.

"I'm coming, buddy," I said. "Hey, guys! I think Charlie found something."

I scrambled up the sloping front yard toward him. He ducked back into the house as I reached what remained of the front porch. Gingerly, I stepped over the broken wood and hauled myself up onto the cracked living room floor. I stood, dusting my hands off on my pant legs, and froze as my gaze landed on what Charlie had discovered.

A circle had been drawn in chalk in the middle of the room. Under the scent of crumbling drywall was something else. It smelled strangely sweet mixed with pine, citrus, and a hint of earthiness. It was distinct from the smells outside, like incense instead of something natural. Around the circle stood candles with a dark liquid dripped over them.

Is that blood? My mouth dried as I stepped closer.

In the center of the circle, a woman lay on her back. Her dark-brown hair streaked with gray hid her face. She was too still. Even from where I stood, I could tell she was dead.

A woman gasped behind me. I spun toward the sound. Izzy stood wide-eyed and staring to my left. She wasn't looking at the woman on the floor. She was looking past me into what remained of the kitchen. She scrambled away, bumping into Lori, who stood only a foot behind her.

Lori grabbed Izzy's arm before she could flee to the front yard. "What is it? What do you see?"

Izzy yanked at her arm, trying to free herself. Lori's fingers gripped harder, digging into her skin.

"Let her go," I said.

Lori dropped Izzy's arm and stepped back. "What did you see?"

"There's two of them." Izzy hugged herself.

Lori's gaze traveled between the dead body on the floor and the empty doorway. A small smile appeared across her lips. "A necromancer?"

Izzy hunched her shoulders.

I stepped up next to Izzy and put my hand on her shoulder, softening my voice. "Can you ask her what she saw? Maybe she can tell us what happened here."

Izzy shook her head. "No. I've never seen anything like this before. They're both dead. I didn't even know ghosts could die. But… both her physical body and whatever ghosts are made of have been killed."

My gaze slipped to my mother's face. She had pulled her bottom lip into her mouth and was chewing on it as her eyes flicked around the space. I recognized that look. The wheels in her head were turning like she was putting together a puzzle. We only had a few minutes before she would disappear into her thoughts and be impossible to reach. I cleared my throat and caught her eye.

While I was loath to do it, I needed answers, and my mother was more likely to have them than anyone else here. "What are you thinking?"

"Dark magic can break almost anything, and this looks dark. Very dark."

Charlie rubbed against my legs. I crouched and picked him up. "Dark magic? I don't think I've heard of that before. It wasn't listed in any of the laws of magic."

Magic only had three laws: Don't make deals with

Outsiders to augment your powers. Don't permanently alter someone's mind, body, or spirit without their informed consent. And lastly, don't violate the natural order.

Lori screwed up her face. "It didn't have to be listed. All dark magic out there violates at least one of the laws." She pointed to the ritual circle. "It doesn't get any more permanent than killing someone. And if your friend's right, it sounds like this one went a step further. I can't think of anything outside of dark magic that could kill a ghost."

"So, it's official then?" I wet my lips, my mouth too dry. "Meredith's out... and someone used dark magic to do it?"

Lori nodded.

I looked between her and Izzy. Then my gaze slid to the front porch, where Megan stood, blocking Grace's view of the body. Chris waited in the roadway beyond them, his phone still plastered to his ear as he continued to give directions to Harrison or Peggy. This was officially too big for us to handle.

My hands shook as I pulled my phone from my pocket.

"What are you doing?" Lori asked.

I turned away from her and dialed. I'd never thought this would be a call I would willingly make. "Calling the Wardens."

CHAPTER 3

I could feel their eyes on me as I raised my phone to my ear.

The line didn't even finish ringing once before Miranda's cool voice filled my ear. "Delaney is already en route. I'm on another assignment. I'll get there when I can. It'll be a few days. Oh, and Miss Williams? Don't do anything stupid before we get there."

The line went dead in my hands. I shoved the phone into my pocket and exhaled slowly in an attempt to steady my breathing. I shuddered at the thought of working with Delaney. Both Wardens gave me the creeps, from Delaney's too-white hair and ageless face to Miranda's sharp features and too-blue eyes. They both had a way of looking at me that made my skin crawl. It was like they could see right through me and knew how to pull my strings. It probably didn't help that the first time I'd met Delaney, she had ambushed me in the middle of the night. And while I'd become accustomed to the somewhat pretty magic that came out of my coven, hers reminded me of Ursula from the *Little Mermaid*. It was all dark and tentacley.

"Dani?" Megan whispered.

I swallowed and turned toward her. "They're on their way."

"All right, then." Megan grabbed her phone. "Hopefully, the Retirees aren't already in bed. It's time for an emergency coven meeting."

I glanced behind her at Chris hovering in the background. He had finished his calls for backup. Sirens blared in the distance. I scrambled down the embankment toward him and came to a stop a few feet away. He reached out to me, and I twined my fingers with his.

Chris rubbed his thumb against the back of my hand. "I know that look."

"There's a body up there," I said.

He pressed his lips together into a thin line and nodded. "Murdered, I assume?"

"Yeah." I glanced at Meredith's house, where the others had stepped out of the wreckage and stood gathered on the lawn. I sighed. "The Wardens are on their way. We need to have a coven meeting."

"Can you—"

"Do you want to come?" I blurted. I didn't know where the question came from. One second, it flitted across my thoughts. The next, I had said it.

He gave a half chuckle. It wasn't amusement. It was shock.

I peered up at him through my eyelashes as the sirens grew louder. "Is that a yes or a no?"

"It's a yes." Chris raised my hand and brushed his lips across my knuckles. "I'm glad you asked. It means a lot that you want to include me. And on a practical front, I want to know everything. I've got a feeling more bodies are about to start dropping. And I can't keep people safe if I'm in the dark."

I opened my mouth to respond as a sheriff's SUV pulled to a stop next to me. I glanced over as Harrison unfolded himself from the vehicle. He was easily one of the tallest people I had ever met at six foot five if not taller. It was hard to tell, because he had a habit of slouching, his thin frame gangly in his uniform. He pushed his blond hair back from his forehead and strode toward us, his long legs eating up the distance in a few strides.

"Any idea what happened here?" Harrison asked.

Chris shrugged. "At first, I thought a gas leak with a spark that made the place blow. But we found a body inside, so now I'm worried about it being a meth lab or something worse. Either way, we've got to secure the scene. Let's cordon off the street so no one can get close and evacuate the homes nearby just in case."

Harrison nodded along to Chris's words, his eyes flicking between me and the other women on the lawn. He chewed his lip and released a long sigh as he rubbed the back of his neck. "Looks like we have a lot of witnesses to interview."

"We do."

"Why don't you, uh, handle that while I secure the scene?"

Chris's shoulders relaxed, and he gave Harrison a small smile. While Harrison didn't know anything about the witch stuff, he knew I was helpful for investigations. It seemed like he wanted to give Chris the opportunity to accept my help without getting involved himself. Smart guy.

Chris squeezed my hand and stepped back. "I'll conduct the interviews someplace a bit less intimidating. Keep me updated."

"Will do, sir." Harrison retreated to his SUV to collect caution tape.

I waved the others over. Megan, with her arm wrapped around Izzy's shoulder, marched toward me. Grace followed, her arms hugging her body, with Charlie trotting at her feet. Lori took up the rear. Even walking across the uneven ground, she was graceful. They all came to a stop and formed a semicircle around me, their eyes expectant.

"To the Bizzy Bean?" I asked.

Wordlessly, we all climbed back into our respective vehicles. Megan followed us in her truck. It was almost ten o'clock at night when we parked outside the cafe. Betty's truck was already parked in front, and the lights were still on in the back. I let myself in with my key and locked the door behind me so any passersby wouldn't see the lights on and assume Heather had changed her hours. The scent of coffee and baked goods eased the tension in my shoulders. I held Chris's hand tightly as we moved into the plexiglass enclosure that kept the cafe's cats away from the food service area. I stepped to the side and let the others file in next to me.

The Retirees huddled in the back booth, forming a line. They were dressed in their usual track suits, tonight's color a pine green. They sat from the whitest hair, Agnes, to the darkest, Sarah. While Betty was mostly salt-and-pepper, Sarah only had one white streak at the front. They raised their eyebrows in unison when they saw Chris at my side. Their mouths dropped into O's at the sight of Izzy, which was immediately replaced by a scowl on Betty's face when her gaze finally landed on my mother. Heather, who had been perched at the end of the booth, went through a similar transformation. But instead of a scowl, her expression went strangely blank—like she was holding her emotions close to her chest.

"I thought this was a private meeting," Betty said.

"It's a coven meeting. Plus a few extras." I tilted my head back.

Sarah eyed Chris a moment longer before her gaze landed back on Izzy. Her eyes bounced back and forth between the three newcomers, like she couldn't decide who she should object to most.

Megan still had her arm over Izzy's shoulders in a protective stance. From the corner of my eye, I could see her hand flexing. After being the town's outcast her whole life, I suspected she was still getting used to voicing her opinions on things in front of so many people. She cleared her throat. "Izzy's a new witch. I didn't want to leave her at home. She has to learn fast. And this is an excellent opportunity."

The Retirees nodded but then looked at Chris again.

I squeezed his hand. "We're getting married. He's going to be a big part of my life moving forward, which means he's a part of this, too, and shouldn't be left out."

Grace gasped next to me and spun toward us. "Since when?"

I flushed. "Earlier this evening. We were on our way to talk to you about it when this all happened." I grimaced. "Are you okay with it?"

Grace released a high-pitched squeal and threw herself at me as she pulled me into a tight hug. "Okay with it? Are you crazy? I couldn't be happier."

Everyone at the booth stood and surged forward to crowd around me and Chris. I was pulled into hug after hug as they all congratulated us. I couldn't make out the individual words as they overlapped. But they were all so joy filled that I couldn't help but grin at the onslaught of affection. Even the horror of Meredith being free couldn't take this moment from me.

Sarah and Agnes released me and returned to the booth. Betty stayed back, her eyes on Lori. We ambled toward the table as a group. Heather reclaimed her spot at the end of the booth, while Izzy, Grace, and Megan found their seats. Chris and I grabbed extra chairs and plopped down to begin the conversation. The entire time, Betty watched Lori. She stalked across the room and slid into her spot, her eyes narrowed. Lori ignored her as she grabbed a chair and pulled it up to the table. She claimed the space on the other side of Chris, as far from me and Betty as she could get.

"I guess we should get started?" Agnes grabbed the salt from the center of the table.

Megan had helped Heather design the booth setup with a resin top and powerful herbs and crystals embedded into it. A silver-and-iron braid had been sunk into the wood in a circle around the table. It had been designed so we could more easily create magical circles to prevent eavesdropping. With the extra chairs pulled up to the table, we had spilled over the metal strip, and to keep the meeting private, we would need to use the old-fashioned method of a salt circle. We wanted to keep the Wardens—the secret police of the witching world—from eavesdropping and hopefully avoid catching their attention when we discussed our issues. However, with them coming into town, I wasn't sure if the secrecy really mattered anymore.

I sighed. "I already called the Wardens. They're on their way."

It was like I had thrown a bucket of ice water over everyone at the table. They all stiffened with a few sharp inhales. The Retirees froze and stared at me. Everyone who had been with me at Meredith's house already knew. But if I didn't explain the call quickly, I was sure it would feel like a betrayal.

"The prison broke. Meredith's free."

More sharp inhales. In a rapid word vomit, I quickly went over what we had found at the house—the green flames, the collapsed living room, the dead body, the dark magic. With each word, the tension at the table grew.

Izzy shifted in her seat. "What does all this mean?"

I exchanged looks with the other women at the table, silently asking permission to share our history. One by one, they nodded, except for Lori, who simply cocked her head and shrugged. I pinched the bridge of my nose and exhaled.

"Who's Meredith? What's a Warden?" Izzy asked.

"It's complicated. It's two big history lessons we don't have the time to completely get into right now. But I'll start with the Wardens then explain *Meredith*." I straightened and drummed my fingers on the table. "Has Megan shared the three laws of magic with you yet?"

Izzy nodded. "Briefly."

I raised my hand and ticked them off. "Thou shalt not permanently alter someone's mind, body, or spirit without their informed consent. Thou shalt not violate the natural order of the world. And thou shalt not make deals with Outsiders to augment your power. Basically, back in the day, some witches made some bad decisions. There was the Inquisition. Yes, the Spanish one, among others, and these laws were decided upon by the witching community to keep us safe. A council was formed of the big movers and shakers, and to make sure the rest of us followed the rules, the Wardens were created. They represent the Witch Council, and to put it mildly, they enforce the laws."

"So, they're like witch police?" Izzy asked.

"They're more than just police. They are also frequently the judge, jury, and executioner," I said.

Sarah nodded along. She was the historian at the table. "So much so that there is an unspoken fourth law: Thou shalt not attract the attention of a warden."

Izzy gulped. "And they're coming here?"

I grimaced. "Yeah."

"Because of Meredith?" Izzy looked around the table.

I fidgeted under her gaze as the rest of the table awkwardly nodded.

"Yeah," I said. "Because of Meredith."

"Meredith was a member of my mother's coven," Agnes said.

"And my mom's too," Betty chimed in.

Sarah leaned forward in her seat. "Every witch at this table, well, except for you, is descended from her coven."

"And that's a bad thing?" Izzy's eyes widened.

I nodded. "Meredith broke every law there was, including making a deal with an Outsider. Her coven was afraid she would catch a Warden's attention. This terrified them. When a Warden comes to town, it's not always just the witch who broke the law that they punish. They punish anyone who could have stopped her, who could have done something about her. So her coven tried to do that. They tried to strip her of her powers so she couldn't break the laws anymore."

I closed my eyes as the vision of the confrontation played through my head. After we had cast the spell to see into the past to figure out what had happened, the vision replayed in my dreams at least once a week. *Traitors.* Her voice had been a mix of anguish and anger. "It didn't go well. She cursed them, and they were forced to bind her to her house."

"That's intense," Izzy murmured. "And I take it she's still got a bone to pick with her jailors? But aren't they dead?"

"She wanted to wipe out everyone she saw as betraying her. Her jailors, everyone related to her jailors... and everyone related to the reason she made the deal with an Outsider to begin with. Everyone related to the men responsible for the death of her lover." I slumped into my seat. "So, most of this table as well as a bunch of guys who had nothing to do with what their great-grandparents did back in the day."

"That sounds like a lot of people," Izzy said.

"It is." I sighed.

"Although, in a strange way, the silver lining of her escaping is that we might finally be able to do something about our curses." Lori set her notebook on the table.

"You're all still cursed?" Izzy asked.

I nodded and pointed to the women around the table, starting with myself. "I have powers of divination. So do my daughter and mom. Our curse is that we can't control it. The visions come whether we want them to or not. Betty's family specialized in transformation magic. Her curse is that everything she casts has some sort of negative, unintended consequence. The bigger the spell, the bigger the consequence.

Because of this, she doesn't cast magic much. Why take the risk? Agnes specializes in illusion magic. Her curse confined her to a single reality. She can't ever leave Point Pleasant without becoming so sick she could die. Sarah's strength is in evocation magic, basically control over the elements. She can only access her magic on the full moon. And Megan is all about charming people, which was twisted into people inherently distrusting her."

"I don't—"

"You can drink a special coffee to mitigate it. So long as you keep up with the doses. If you miss one, all the distrust comes back all at once." I drummed my fingers on the table. "Any other questions?"

"Who were the men?" Izzy asked.

"Harold and James Mitchell, Thomas Reynolds, Benjamin Hayes, and George Wright." I ticked their names off on my fingers.

Izzy gasped. "Benjamin Hayes? He started the paper I used to work at."

Chris squeezed my hand. "He used his clout to cover up his friends' misdeeds. If it didn't make the news, it couldn't possibly be real, right?"

"Wow." Izzy sagged into her seat. "He gave his life to that paper. I don't remember hearing about him having a family at all."

"He never married," I said.

"Well, that's at least one line of descendants we don't have to worry about. What about the others?" Izzy asked.

Chris straightened in his seat. He had handled the arrest of Harold Mitchell and Benjamin Hayes for the murder of Booker Lancaster, Meredith's lover, six months prior. He knew more about the five men involved than anyone else. "Harold was the ringleader. He was the closest this town came to organized crime. He inherited a rum-running business from his dad and built himself an empire—well, a

Whidbey Island–sized empire. Meredith was his girl for a while, and he took it as a personal offense when she broke things off with him to begin a relationship with Booker Lancaster, known as Beau to his friends. He killed Booker, which, from what I understand, is what sent Meredith down the whole revenge, making-deals-with-an-Outsider path. He didn't act alone, though. His whole group of friends either helped with the act or helped cover it up. Harold's brother, James, was originally the muscle of the group. They had a falling out, and James became the opposite. From all accounts, when he passed, he was a pillar of the community and a stand-up guy. He only has one descendant, Jay Mitchell."

I nodded along. "Jay's dad was killed almost eight months ago. I, uh… may have helped clear Jay's name when he became a suspect."

Izzy's gaze bounced between us, her eyes wide as she tried to absorb the onslaught of information.

Chris cleared his throat and continued. "You know Benjamin already. He owned the paper. He refused to publish anything about Booker's disappearance. Thomas Reynolds was the group's attorney. He handled all the legal paperwork to steal Booker's home out from under his family. Thomas had two sons. The oldest is Kevin, and the youngest was Adrian."

I nodded. Only a few days prior, the Outsider had possessed a dead body and tried to hunt down the descendants. It had successfully taken out Adrian Reynolds, but Izzy and I had managed to stop it before it could kill Kevin.

"And the last of the group was George Wright, one of the deputies at the time. He used his position to avoid an investigation." Chris paused for a second. His next words caught in his throat. "His son, Bob, is the current sheriff. My boss."

Bob was more than just his boss. Despite being my part-time nemesis, he was Chris's mentor. While I didn't like him, he wasn't a bad guy. If Bob died, it would wreck Chris. I squeezed his hand under the table.

"Any other questions?" I asked.

Izzy shook her head, but Betty leaned forward and pointed at Lori. "Why is *she* here?"

Lori tapped the top of her notebook. "To bring this. It's filled with everything I know about the curse and how to break it."

Betty scoffed.

Sarah put her hand on Betty's arm and cleared her throat. "You've said you knew how to break it before. It didn't work then."

Lori's eyes gleamed with passion as she gripped the notebook. "It didn't. But this time, I have two decades of visions and prophecies to back me up. I've spent years dissecting everything I see, learning the steps, and figuring out how necromancy works so we can pull this off. It's no easy feat. But it's all in here. I know what to do now. I won't have another false start."

My stomach roiled, and my heart clenched. Every fiber of my being wanted to trust her, but we had been burned too many times in the past. Opening my mouth felt like forcing myself to step barefoot onto hot coals. "Okay. What do we have to do?"

Lori flipped her notebook open, her finger gliding from page to page. It was filled with her neat handwriting. I recognized it from the notes she had added to my grandmother's journals.

She tapped her finger on the center of the page and smiled. "There's a ritual, of course. I've seen it enough that I could write it all down. It'll take time to prepare everything. I'll go through the individual steps later, but the long and short of it is we need the descendants from all the witches involved in the curse to be there to confront Meredith. We'll need a charm to lure her to us. Next, we'll need to use necromancy to rebind her spirit, then we'll go through a third ritual that will help her rest peacefully. Her current bonds prevent her from doing that."

"So, you need a necromancer?" Izzy asked.

Lori shook her head. "Only witches descended from that original cursed coven can participate. I've been practicing necromancy for years. I'm confident I can do it. We just need —" Her head jerked to the side as she looked back over the women at the table. "Where's Kim?"

"She's not part of the coven," I said.

"In my visions, Kim is always there. She has to be." Lori's hands clenched in front of her.

Megan put her hand over Lori's, her voice gentle. "After the last time we failed, Kim left the coven."

Lori gaped. "Does she even know what's going on?"

"Some of it," I said. "We're barely on speaking terms."

"But she *has* to be there. She is there. I've seen it. I've dreamed it." Lori clutched at the sides of her head. "If she isn't there, it won't work. It has to work. If I just explain, she'll come. I know it. I know she'll help."

"It will be hard to convince her," Megan said.

Lori rocked back and forth in her seat. "She'll join us. We'll convince her before the next full moon."

"I don't—"

Lori cut me off as she stood from the table. "I've seen it. She'll be there."

Megan sighed and stood. "We might as well try to convince her now. There's no way she missed those green flames. She's probably expecting us to show up. And the longer we let her sit and wait, the more time she'll have to come up with arguments against helping."

My legs shook as I pushed myself to my feet. "You're probably right. Let's go convince Kimberly Jones to join the fight."

CHAPTER 4

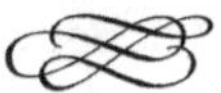

I hadn't been to Kimberly Jones's house in months. It was a rambler-style house, with a wide driveway to the side of it. A path wound from the driveway to the front door. The yard was a riot of color. Chrysanthemums and pansies lined the walkway. She had repainted the siding since I last visited. It was a soft cream color with navy-blue trim. I parked my car behind Betty's truck, and we all shuffled out of our vehicles. I could feel the magic in the air before I stepped onto the path. It was electric but not unpleasant. I had made it two steps up the path when Kimberly's front door slammed open, and she stepped out onto her front step.

Kimberly leaned on her forearm crutches as she glared at the group of women clustered on her driveway. "Just because I agreed to help put down the warning alarm on Meredith's prison doesn't mean I'm willing to go any further. Back up. Turn around. And find someone else."

Lori pushed past me. "It isn't anyone else who helps. It's you. I've *seen* it."

Kimberly scoffed and lifted one of her crutches. I didn't know the details, but from what I'd heard, the last time Lori had been in town to tackle the curse, Kimberly had agreed to help, and things had gone wrong. Whatever had happened had made her need to use those crutches for the rest of her life.

Kimberly was descended from the same coven, and her curse was the nastiest of the bunch. Her specialty was protection magic, and it had been twisted against her as well, making her body weak. Her bones were so fragile that she could break her leg simply by crossing the room. And once broken, her bones never healed. Twenty years ago, she had shattered the femurs in both legs, and they were still fractured. If she didn't use magic every second of every day to maintain the spells holding herself together, she would either break further or die.

Whatever had gone down the last time, her concentration had faltered. The protection spells had dropped for a minute, and she'd broken. I didn't blame her for being unwilling to put herself on the line again. But if my mother was right, it was in her best interest to get involved.

Gritting my teeth, I stepped around my mother, blocking her view of Kimberly. "I wish we didn't have to come here. I do. But, Kimberly… I don't think any of us has a choice."

"Of course I do. And I'm choosing no." Kimberly stepped backward into her house.

I surged forward, trying to catch her eye before she closed the door in our faces. "Meredith won't care that you want to be left alone. She only cares that you descended from someone who wronged her. She will come for you."

Kimberly held my eyes for a few seconds before looking away. "I know how to keep myself safe."

I chewed on the inside of my cheek. Kimberly was a lot like me. She was a mother who worked tirelessly to keep her family safe. The idea of Grace getting hurt again terrified me. A twinge of guilt shot through me as I opened my mouth to push the only button I knew would get us through that door. "Do your kids know how to keep themselves safe?"

I tried to catch Kimberly's eyes again, but her gaze darted away.

Her tongue flicked out, licking the corner of her lip. "I can keep them safe too. I'll put up more wards."

I inched forward and softened my voice, speaking as one mother to another. "And keep them prisoner in their own home?"

Kimberly stiffened at the word "prisoner."

I took another half step forward. "Meredith won't just go away, not unless we do something about it."

Kimberly's jaw clenched, and she turned her stare toward me. Her blue eyes held a fire. "Do you even have a plan?"

Somehow, I had missed Lori inching up behind me. She stepped around me, holding up her notebook. "I do. If we all work together, we can put her to rest. We can break the curse. We'll be free. But we can only do it if all the descendants from her coven come together to perform the ritual."

Kimberly shifted on her feet and leaned more heavily on her crutches. "If that's the case, we'll have to wait until the full moon to break it. Sarah won't be any help until then."

Lori and Kimberly opened their mouths to continue the conversation. I could sense my mother trying to push for an invitation inside, while Kimberly was preparing to tell us to come back in three days' time. But I knew we didn't have three days to sit on our hands. Meredith was out now.

I darted forward, putting myself between the two women and blurted, "Meredith can cause a lot of chaos in that time."

Kimberly blinked.

"She isn't just coming after us. She's coming after the descendants of the men who wronged her. And they're innocent." I took the last step toward Kimberly, stopping in front of her, the tips of my shoes pressed against the bottom step. I stared up at her and poured all my conviction into the next sentence. "We have to work together to contain her, to protect those who can't protect themselves."

Kimberly sighed and took another step back. She turned away and walked into her house, leaving her front door open. "Then you better come inside before I change my mind."

I scrambled after her. Lori followed close on my heels then Heather, Megan, Grace, Chris, and the Retirees. Charlie wound his way around our legs and skipped ahead to stand beside me in Kimberly's living room. It was large, with a plush sectional couch taking up the center of the room.

Kimberly stood in the doorway to the dining room, her eyes bouncing from face to face. She gripped the handles of her crutches, her hands shaking. "You might as well sit down."

One by one, everyone found a place to sit. I perched on the armrest next to Chris. The room was silent as everyone turned to stare at me. My mouth dried as the realization hit that they all expected me to say something, to lead the meeting.

I stood and rubbed my sweaty palms against my pant legs. "Thank you all for agreeing to work together. As I said, Meredith could cause a lot of chaos in the next few days. She isn't just coming after us. She's also coming after Kevin, Bob…" My mind floundered as I tried to recall all the names I knew. Most of them were already dead. As it was, Kevin was lucky to be alive. The last time the Outsider had struck, it had attacked Kevin in his home, and he had barely escaped. I focused, and my thoughts landed on the last name I knew for sure. Jay Mitchell. He was the same age as my daughter. "And Jay. I know there are probably more than that. We'll have to dig deep to find those names so we can warn them."

Chris cleared his throat. "I think I can help with that."

Every face turned toward him.

He was the only man in the room, and he wasn't a witch. He must have felt so out of place. He didn't acknowledge the strangeness. Instead, he plowed forward with his plan. "I have access to a more complete list. I don't have the names on me, but the last person who worked with the Outsider wrote them down. Julie? She had other names on the list, too, so I'll have to figure out which ones were for the Outsider and which were part of her revenge plot. But I can get it."

"That's great, my love." I squeezed his shoulder. "Now we just need to warn the descendants we do know about. I think if we can convince them to leave town, we can buy some time until we tackle the real issue. Meredith."

"I can help with that too," Chris said. "I'll call them under the pretense that their names appeared on the list. I can argue that we want to make sure Julie wasn't working with anyone else and it might be best if they lie low for a few days while we do our due diligence."

I nodded, and he stood. He pulled his phone out of his pocket and moved past Kimberly into the dining room to start making calls.

With that taken care of, my mind whirled. *What next? Do we try to temporarily rebind her? How do we even track her down?*

"Do we know who Meredith's accomplice was this time?" Heather asked. "I mean, now that Julie is behind bars, waiting for her trial to start. And why this woman? Who was she? Did any of you recognize her?"

I exchanged a look with Megan, Grace, Lori, and Izzy. We had all seen the victim, but I had been too distracted by the ritual circle to take a closer look at her face. She hadn't stood out as someone I knew, though. We all shook our heads, one by one. None of us knew her.

Was it a case of the wrong place at the wrong time? Or was she important somehow? My shoulders dropped. I had too many questions.

"I don't know the answer to either question. I could try to go back to Meredith's house to perform some divination rituals." I grimaced. The last time I'd used divination magic in an area affected by the Outsider or Meredith's necromancy magic, it hadn't gone well. It gave me a serious case of nausea, and I could barely focus on the spell. While I did finally see something useful, it took a while. And her house was probably crawling with cops.

"All right. Chris can probably take the lead on identifying the woman. Knowing Harrison, he's already working on it. So, let's focus on the magical aspect. I'll just go out on a limb here and assume it was the fragment of the Outsider that released her. Last time, it used a dead body to do the dirty work. Maybe it's using another one?" Megan suggested.

I nodded. "Sounds reasonable. We should look into all the recent deaths in the area to see if any were particularly vengeful. I think that was a necessary component. Kindred spirits and all that."

We all pulled out our phones and searched the local news sites. I started with the *Island County Gazette,* reading through the crime section. The Retirees claimed the obituaries, and everyone else claimed other local news sources. We called out names as we found them. With each name, the group would pause as we read the article aloud. By the end of our sleuthing, we had a list of three names that might fit the bill. Graham Pritchard, age thirty-seven, drowned fully clothed in his bathtub. Irene Hensley, age forty-two, died from a painkiller overdose. And Nadia Dupree, age twenty-one, had an unknown cause of death. Her social media account was full of flame wars and infighting with her sorority sisters. They all felt like deaths that would make someone resentful. Not that any death couldn't breed resentment. Losing someone never felt fair. But those stood out above the rest.

I stretched and stood from my spot on the end of the couch. "It looks like all three were buried at different cemeteries. Why don't we split up? We'll cover more ground that way."

"Sounds like a plan." Megan yawned. "I'll take Bakersfield."

"I'll come with you," Kimberly offered.

"Me too," Lori said.

Kimberly ground her teeth. "No. While I may not hate you, that doesn't mean I trust you to have my back."

Tension hung in the air as I looked around the room. Chris was still preoccupied, leaving nine of us here. We could easily split up into groups of three, but as I looked around, the other women shifted awkwardly away from Lori. It wouldn't be a comfortable split.

I pinched the bridge of my nose. "Okay. Fair enough, Kimberly. I get why you don't want to go with Lori right now. Who here would like to team up with her?"

I glanced around the room. No one moved.

"Okay… Who here feels comfortable teaming up with her?"

Sarah, Agnes, and Grace all raised their hands. I tried to hide my glower at Grace's raised hand. She didn't know Lori like I did, so I couldn't hold her willingness against her.

Heather stood and squeezed my shoulder. "How about Dani, Betty, and Izzy take Garden Terrace? Grace, Megan, and Kim, you can take Bakersfield. And Lori, Sarah, and Agnes can take the one on Memorial Way."

The Retirees bristled but kept their mouths shut as they jerkily nodded. Separating Betty from her lifelong friends felt strange. But it made sense keeping her with me and Izzy. While Betty didn't use magic often, her knowledge far outpaced my own, and she could give guidance to us in the field.

"What group will you go with?" I asked.

Heather blinked. "Oh, um. Yours? I guess I thought you needed witch powers to detect the bad stuff."

"Maybe? But another pair of eyes to check for disturbed graves would be helpful," I said.

Heather pressed her lips together, nodded, and grabbed her purse. "I'm ready whenever you are."

I turned to the rest of the room, making eye contact with each of the women. "Are we good?"

I received a chorus of unenthusiastic yeses.

"Then let's head out." I glanced toward the kitchen.

Chris was still on the phone. I ducked my head in and whispered a quick update to him.

He followed me out as he grunted into the line, "Hold on a sec." Chris lowered the phone and kissed me. "I'll meet back up with Harrison at the scene. He messaged, saying he found something. I'll text you when I'm done. Keep me updated?"

"Will do. Love you." I kissed him back.

He smiled against my mouth. "Love you too."

My heart was fluttering as I climbed into my car. It still felt new saying those words. But I carried them with me like armor as I drove toward the cemetery. I didn't know if I hoped to find something or not. I really wanted Irene to be resting peacefully, but either way, Chris's love fueled me as I drove toward the unknown.

CHAPTER 5

A stone settled in my stomach as I stared at the gate for Garden Terrace Cemetery across the street. It had only been a matter of days since I'd been there last. My showdown with Justin lingered in my head—the way he'd moved, like a puppet on a string, the wrongness about it. Being so close had made me nauseous. I swallowed, tasting bile at the back of my throat. *Am I queasy because something's wrong again, or is it just the memory of it?* I focused on my body. It was hard to tell. I didn't feel the overwhelming urge to vomit like I had last time I was here. *Maybe I'm not close enough?*

"You ready?" Heather asked.

I nodded and got out of the car. Betty, Izzy, and Heather followed suit. We gathered in front of my car and stared for a few more seconds at the open gate. The sun had set hours ago. It was inching its way toward midnight. I popped the trunk of my car and rummaged in the kit I kept there for home inspections. I pulled out my flashlight and a few of my backup flashlights and handed them out. The beams of light illuminated the road in front of us, making the rest of the street darker in comparison. I swallowed and pressed forward, the other women clustering in around me as we marched toward the gate.

No matter what, visiting a cemetery late at night was creepy. The moon was almost full overhead, but it was half covered by clouds, leaving the grounds dimly lit. I could make out the shapes of tombstones scattered throughout. My eyes focused on the path in front of me, my flashlight arcing back and forth between the rows. Every few steps, I glanced from side to side, following the arc with my eyes. Tombstone after tombstone, the ground remained undisturbed.

After ten minutes, we made it to the end of the first row. I had turned left and took a step to walk down the second row of graves when Heather's hand darted out and stopped me.

"We'll be at it all night at this rate," she said.

I shrugged. "It has to be done."

"Why don't we split up?" Izzy asked.

I turned toward them. "It's not—"

Heather squeezed my shoulder. "We don't have to separate far. We can even go in pairs. Walking two rows at a time instead of just one will be faster."

"Fine." I glanced between the other women. Heather wasn't a witch, so she couldn't cast spells to defend herself. And Betty's curse made it so she didn't want to. The risks were too great. I chewed on my lip as I ran through the options in my head. If we wanted to separate, we needed to do it intelligently. "Izzy and Betty, you take the next row. I'll team up with Heather."

Without a word, we split up. Heather looped her arm through mine, and we started back down the second row. I focused my beam of light to the right, and she focused on the left. Her fingers dug into my arm as we padded down the row. At the end, we turned, walked up two rows to skip the one Izzy and Betty checked, and continued.

The farther into the cemetery we walked, the older the headstones became. A few newer ones were interspersed as families expanded their plots. But scattered here and there were some from the founding of the town, the text old and crumbling. The trees grew wider with age, their branches thicker overhead. With each step, twigs snapped under foot.

Heather jumped and pulled me closer. She pointed her flashlight at a bush, her finger thrust toward it. "Something moved."

I stared at the bush, pulling on my power. I could feel it humming under my skin, prepared for me to open my mouth and fling my will at whatever lurked in the darkness. Nothing moved. I steadied my breathing and focused on my body. My heart raced, but it could have been from Heather's alarm. The hair on my arms and neck lay flat, and while the pressure at the back of my head slowly pulsed as my divination abilities tried to warn me of something important, the sensation hadn't changed since we'd turned down this aisle. There was no nausea. Whatever Heather had seen move wasn't undead.

She inched away from me toward the bush and crouched, peering between the branches. Her shoulders slumped, and she rocked back on her heels. "It's just a raccoon."

I held my hand out to her and hauled her back to her feet. She looped her arm in mine again, and we turned back to the aisleway.

Other than the one grave we knew would be disturbed, nothing was out of place. No lingering spots made me nauseous, and when I relaxed my eyes to look for signs of magic, the ground was clear of it. Nothing sinister had happened there since my last visit. If the Outsider was possessing another dead body, it wasn't Irene's.

"I didn't notice anything weird. You guys?" I asked when we regrouped.

Izzy's eyes flicked from side to side, her shoulders hunched. "Other than a few ghosts? No."

I stiffened. "Are you okay?"

Izzy sighed and rubbed at her face. I had been so focused on my search with Heather that I hadn't registered her discomfort until now.

"I'll be fine. I just need to tell Louise Saintclaire that her wedding ring is in the blue jar on the second shelf and check in with the local shelter to make sure Mr. Pickles was adopted by a good family."

"Mr. Pickles?" My eyebrows rose.

"Bellamy's cat. He's very concerned." Izzy glanced to the side. "Yes, I will come back and let you know how Mr. Pickles is doing. You don't need to come with me."

I grimaced. Poor Izzy. As probably the only person in town capable of seeing ghosts, she was inundated with their requests. Ignoring them didn't do her any good. Ghosts typically couldn't leave the area where they died or were buried unless something else was anchoring them. Sometimes, it was a physical object, like the murder weapon. They couldn't move far from one of their anchors. The only exception was if they were lucky enough to cross paths with a medium or a necromancer. People who could speak with the dead acted as living anchors, and ghosts could freely follow them. That meant they flocked to her and would harass her until she fixed whatever problem they had. As a new witch, she probably found it exhausting.

"I didn't see anything either," Betty said. "Let's check in with the girls and hopefully wrap this up for tonight."

I nodded and pulled out my phone as we made our way back to my car. Chris had texted me twenty minutes ago.

> **CHRIS:**
> I couldn't get ahold of Bob. I'm swinging by his house to check on him.

I stumbled to a stop as I read the next message. It was sent two minutes ago.

> **CHRIS:**
> He wasn't home. I can't find him, and he still isn't answering his phone.

My heart stuttered, and my hands clamped around my phone. *Bob's missing.* I didn't like the guy. He had been a stumbling block to so many of my investigations. He had arrested me for interfering in one of his. But he... was missing. My mind immediately went to Chris. They had worked together for years. Even with their differences over me, he still looked up to the guy. Once upon a time, Chris had been his protégé. And now he was unaccounted for, with a vengeful ghost out there who wanted to kill him. *What if he's already dead?*

CHAPTER 6

I sprinted for the car. *Don't be dead. Don't be dead. Please. I know we didn't get along, but don't you dare be dead.*

"Where are you going?" Betty yelled after me.

"Bob's missing!" I didn't miss a beat. I kept running, my legs propelling me across the road.

Betty cursed and ran after me. She was surprisingly fast from all the years she had spent power walking. She caught up to me easily and ran at my side the rest of the way. I skidded to a stop, unlocked my car, and yanked the door open in one smooth motion. I threw myself across the front seat and pulled out the collection of maps I kept stowed away in the glove compartment. I tossed them down onto the hood of my car and began to mutter the words to a tracking spell. Bob was Bob. While I couldn't use tracking spells to find a person, I could use it to find objects, and if I knew one thing about Bob, it was that he didn't go anywhere without his badge.

My words were urgent. Motes of light flew out of my mouth faster than they ever had before and landed on the map, highlighting an area just outside of town. I leaned forward. On this map, it wasn't labeled, but I knew the area.

He was at the sheriff's station—or at least where it was temporarily located. The historic sheriff's station downtown was currently being renovated after a massive water leak had made the whole department evacuate it a few years prior. The renovations were almost complete. They would be moving back in within a few weeks. But for now, the sheriff's department was still housed in a few double-wides at the edge of town.

Without a word, we all climbed into the car. I tossed my phone to Heather as I pulled away from the curb. "Tell Chris that Bob's at the sheriff's station."

I gripped the steering wheel as we drove in silence. *Don't you dare be dead.* My shoulders were raised almost to my ears. Tension ran through my body as the minutes ticked by. *Why are we so far away? Why didn't I check my phone earlier?* I berated myself the entire drive back into town for missing Chris's text.

"Chris is thirty minutes out," Heather said.

I nodded and pushed my foot a little harder onto the gas. The streets were empty as I flew through town. My car squealed to a stop only a few feet from the temporary sheriff's station. I jumped out of the vehicle and barreled toward the front door, my feet pounding up the ramp. The double-wides had seen better days. They weren't intended to be used for so many years. The paint had peeled under the sun. The metal skirting around the bases of the buildings had blown off in a storm three years back and had never been replaced. Moss covered the rocks underneath and crept across the gravel that surrounded the structure on all four sides. I barely registered that the lights were out when I hit the front door. It didn't open under my hand. I pounded against it.

"Bob! Bob? Are you in there?" My voice was panicked. I stumbled over my words as I hit the door with my fist.

Chris had been stressed for months over how Bob was

holding up after we uncovered his father's corruption. If Bob was dead, it would devastate Chris.

"Are you sure he's in there?" Heather asked.

I stumbled back from the door. The pressure at the back of my head pulsed stronger by the second. My divination powers screamed that something was wrong. Something bad had happened, and I hadn't stopped it. *He's dead. He's dead. This will wreck Chris. He doesn't deserve to lose his mentor this way. Bob doesn't deserve to die this way. No one does.*

"Dani?" Heather put her hand on my shoulder. "Are you sure he's in there? There are no cars."

I looked behind me at the parking lot. My vehicle was still on, the front door open. But the rest of the parking lot was empty.

"Cast the spell again," Betty suggested.

I slowed my breathing. It was difficult with the pressure building at the back of my head. Something bad had happened—or was happening. I closed my eyes and focused. *You don't know anything yet. Stop panicking.* I exhaled slowly through my mouth and inhaled through my nose again. My heart rate slowed, and my shoulders relaxed. With my body under control, I cast the tracking spell again. This time, I used a variation for tracking something in the vicinity. Motes of light swirled from my mouth and formed a path in front of me that led straight inside the building.

"Well… that answers that question." Betty hugged her arms to her body. "Izzy? Can you hear anything inside?"

Izzy shuffled forward and pressed her ear against the door. She pulled back and shook her head.

"Okay. So he's probably not a ghost, then. I can't imagine a ghost Bob would be any quieter than living Bob." Betty studied the door. "Unless the ghost is dead, too, like that woman was back at Meredith's house."

My stomach clenched. I wasn't sure how a dead ghost

could even happen. *How do you kill a ghost?* It felt wrong on so many levels.

We stood together, studying the door. Betty had worked as a locksmith when she was younger, so we could get in. I grimaced. The idea of breaking and entering into a sheriff's station also felt wrong. If Bob was alive and well, then Chris would have a hard time explaining this to the rest of the department. I was on the verge of asking her to do it anyway when another vehicle pulled into the parking lot. I spun in place, my heart skipping another beat as Chris stepped out of his vehicle.

I vibrated with anxious energy as he strode toward us. He ducked and gave my forehead a quick kiss before slipping past me to the door. He unlocked it, pushed it in, and took the lead, entering first. The waiting area was filled with uncomfortable plastic chairs, a drooping bulletin board, and Peggy's desk. She had worked as the department's office manager for years. Motes of light streamed through the room and disappeared down the hallway.

"Can you see anyone?" I asked Izzy.

She shook her head.

I followed the lights, my feet dragging as I crept closer to the doorway the line swerved into. It was Chris's office. My heart raced, and my palms were sweaty. I wiped my hands on my pant legs as I moved. *Please be okay.* I swallowed and turned the corner. The line ended at Chris's desk. It hovered over the center of the desk. I stared blankly forward, my jaw open. Bob's badge and gun sat in the middle of the desk, an envelope propped on top with one word written across it: *Chris*.

I stumbled forward and picked up the letter. The pressure at the back of my head pulsed, putting black spots on my vision. Chris stepped up next to me, and I handed him the envelope. He slipped out a piece of paper, his brow furrowing as he read. I studied him as waves of sadness rolled off him. He closed his eyes and handed the paper to me.

To: Acting Sheriff Chris Harris
From: Sheriff Robert Wright
Subject: Formal Notice of Resignation

Chris,

I'm not one for long speeches or poetic goodbyes, so I'll keep this simple.

Effective immediately, I'm stepping down as sheriff of Point Pleasant.

I've worn this badge a long damn time. Most days, it meant something good, something solid. But with the truths that have recently come to light, there are things I cannot ignore—not about the job but about the man I thought raised me right. Turns out the foundation I built everything on was a little more rotten than I cared to see.

I've lost a lot over the years. My wife. My boy. And now, I suppose, the last illusion I had left. I always told myself being the sheriff meant something—something bigger than me. Maybe it still does. But I need to find out who I am without this uniform on my back. Before it swallows me whole.

You're a good man, Chris. Smart. Steady. The kind of officer I wish I'd had around when I was younger. I've seen the way you handle things—with heart but without letting it cloud your judgment. That matters.

Don't make the same mistake I did. Don't let the job define you. Protect this town, but don't lose yourself to it. We need more than just lawmen—we need people who remember who they are when the badge comes off.

I've left the files in order. It's your town now.

Make it better than I did.

—Bob

My mouth was dry as I stared at the words on the page. It didn't make sense. But at the same time, it did. Being the sheriff was all Bob cared about. And the reason he became a sheriff, following in his father's footsteps, had been based on a lie. His father wasn't an honorable man. He was a crook. I dropped the letter onto the desk and began to pace. *He's retired. He's left. But has he left town? Is he still in danger? How am I supposed to find him now?*

Chris stopped me in my tracks on my third rotation. He pulled me into a hug, resting his chin on top of my head. "I'll find him. Don't worry."

"How?"

"It's part of my job, isn't it?" He stroked my hair.

"Finding missing people?"

"Uh-huh. I'll find him."

"How?" I croaked.

"All right. You really want to know? I'm going to ask Peggy. She knows him too well. I doubt he could hide from her for long."

I sniffled and pulled back. Heather had snuck into the room while Chris held me. She was reading through the resignation letter. She handed it off to Betty. The letter made the rounds, with Izzy being the last to read it. When Betty handed it off, she cursed and slumped into the chair in front of Chris's desk.

"Now what?" Izzy asked.

I straightened and wiped my face. I mentally went through the options. Bob never carried anything else on him at all times. I couldn't track him. I would have to rely on Chris and Peggy. That left me feeling queasy. The only hope I had was for a prophetic dream, but those were inconsistent. I glanced at the desk, my gaze lingering on the badge. *Unless...* "Can I take his badge with me?"

Chris rocked back on his heels. "What for?"

"If I have an object close to me, and something bad is

going to happen to its owner, I sometimes can get a heads-up through a dream," I said. "It's not foolproof, but it's the closest I've come to directing when I will see something useful."

Chris handed me the badge.

We turned from the room and trudged back out to the cars. Chris looped his arm around my shoulders and pulled me into a side hug as we walked. "Harrison managed to ID the victim. She was a local translator named Jennifer Moore. We're working on tracking down her son. He's studying abroad in Edinburgh right now, so it might take a bit to get ahold of him."

I nodded, my mind still focused on the badge in my hand.

"I've also got some good news and some bad news." Chris paused as we stopped in front of my car. "Good news is there's a potential witness."

I perked up at that, a smile tugging at the corners of my lips. I opened my mouth to speak, but he shook his head.

"The bad news is, she's unconscious. Based on where she was found, it looks like she would have had a clear line of sight into Meredith's living room. And she was close enough to get knocked out by whatever exploded out of the foundation. She was taken to the hospital, and last I heard, she still hasn't woken up."

"Can we visit her tomorrow?" I asked.

He rubbed my arms. "Yeah. Tomorrow. Hopefully, she'll be awake by then."

"Thank you." I rose onto my tiptoes and kissed him. "I really appreciate you working with me on this."

Chris kissed me back. "If I don't, more bodies are going to drop. I've got to protect this town, remember?"

Betty cleared her throat. "Did the other groups find anything?"

I pulled out my phone and texted the group.

DANI:
Checking in. We didn't find anything at Garden Terrace. How about you guys?

MEGAN:
Nothing at Bakersfield.

SARAH:
Nothing at Memorial Way.

DANI:
Regroup in the morning?

MEGAN:
Sure thing. I'll drop Grace off at your place.

DANI:
I still have Izzy with me. Why don't we meet at the Bizzy Bean and trade passengers?

Megan gave my suggestion a thumbs-up.

I pushed my phone into my pocket and turned to Chris. "Do you mind dropping Betty off at her home?"

Chris nodded. We exchanged one more kiss before climbing into our respective vehicles. I tucked Bob's badge into my purse. My eyes flicked to it occasionally as I drove back into town. I wasn't sure how it had happened. Bob was basically my nemesis. But right now, it was hard to focus on anything but mine and Chris's worry. His concern had seeped into me at the sheriff's station, and I wasn't ready to shake it off. We were getting married. His worries were my worries. *Please don't be dead.* I worried my lip as I drove in silence. I tried to center myself by making a list of things to do: Find Bob. Figure out who killed Jennifer Moore. Prepare for the ritual. Banish Meredith. I replayed the list over and over.

Find Bob.

Figure out who killed Jennifer Moore.

Prepare for the ritual.
Banish Meredith.
Find Bob...

CHAPTER 7

I didn't sleep well. My eyes were still heavy as I climbed out of the car and shuffled toward the hospital behind Chris. He had woken me up just after six a.m. with an invitation to join him in his witness interview. With only a few hours of sleep, I couldn't focus on what questions I should ask, so instead, I focused on my feet as I trudged after Chris toward the nurses' station. I stopped a few feet behind him as he flashed his badge.

"I'm here to see Emily Park," he said.

A blue cap with dancing elephants covered the nurse's hair. She frowned and typed a few words into her system. "Mrs. Park is still unconscious."

Chris tapped his badge on the counter, his shoulders hunching.

"Her husband, Jacob, is in the room with her right now. He might be willing to talk."

Chris tapped his badge again and put it away. "Thank you."

She gave him directions to the room. I followed him. I picked at my cuticles as we moved down the hall. It was a long time to be unconscious. *What if she doesn't wake up?* I gritted my teeth and shook the negative thoughts from my head. I would find another thread to pull. *This isn't the only path forward. Think.*

We paused outside the room. I peered inside at Emily Park. She looked small, lying in the center of the large hospital bed. Her chestnut hair spilled across the pillow under her head. Her face was soft. She looked peaceful. I saw no sign of injury from where I stood. Seated next to her, with his back to the door, was a man. His broad shoulders were slumped into the chair, his head tilted back. His cropped black hair stood at odd angles, as if he had run his fingers through it one too many times. His arm was straight out, his fingers looped through hers. From the doorway, I could hear him murmuring something, but it was too quiet to make out. Watching him felt like an intrusion.

I stepped back, my mind too mushy to think of any questions. I wouldn't be effective going into that room, and my presence could detract from the situation. I stepped to the side and leaned against the wall. "I'll wait out here."

Chris nodded then knocked on the door. "Mr. Park? I'm Deputy Chris Harris. I was wondering if you had a few minutes to talk."

The door closed behind Chris. I closed my eyes and leaned against the wall. Now that I wasn't in the room, my heart rate picked up. *What if he says something important and I miss it?* Grumbling under my breath, I smoothed my hands down my sides. I exhaled slowly and murmured the words to the spell that would heighten my senses. Everything hit me like a freight train. A strong disinfectant smell filled my nose. The buzz of fluorescent lights intermixed with crying and machines beeping in other rooms almost overwhelmed me. Luckily, I had changed most of my wardrobe for soft clothing that didn't have awkward, painful seams when my senses were heightened. Touch was my only comfortable sense. I shifted through the sensations until I could focus on the voices in the room next to me.

"—in a coma. I thought if I sat and talked to her, she might recognize my voice and wake up." Jacob's voice was hoarse, like he had been talking for hours.

"I'm sure it will help her," Chris said.

"You said you had questions?"

"I wondered if you saw anything yourself that night."

"I was taking a shower, getting ready for bed. I didn't even know she had left the house. She was downstairs. I don't know why she was out there that late. I—" His voice broke as he sobbed. "Oh god. It's my fault. It's all my fault."

A strange creak followed. "It's going to be okay."

Something clattered loudly in the room. Jacob's voice rose steadily, each word more hysterical than the last. "It's my fault. I forgot to take out the trash. If only I had remembered—she wouldn't have been outside. She would have been in bed. She would be awake right now."

"There's no way to know what would have happened. It's not your fault."

I squeezed my eyes closed as the man's sobs echoed into the hallway. They were so loud, I didn't need the spell. I debated dropping it to give him privacy, but I couldn't, not if he knew something important.

"It's going to be okay," Chris repeated.

Another strange creaking sound followed. *Is he sitting back down?*

"Would you mind calling me when she wakes up?" Chris asked.

"If she—"

"When," Chris cut in.

The man hiccupped. "Okay. When she wakes up, I'll ask her to call you."

I dropped the spell as Chris slipped out into the hallway. He held his hand out to his side, and I twined my fingers through his. We walked back to the parking lot, hand in hand.

"The husband didn't see anything," Chris said.

"I heard."

Chris grunted in acknowledgment. "I've got to go to work today. I'll update you if I find anything useful."

"Same."

We stopped in front of our cars, and he pulled me into a hug, resting his forehead against mine, touching the tip of his nose to mine. He sighed. "I wish we had more time to celebrate. It's not every day someone proposes to me."

I wrapped my arms around him. "I know. But duty calls, and we both have obligations. Love you."

"Love you too."

Saying the words still made me feel giddy, but hearing them made me feel warm and fuzzy, like he had wrapped me in a cozy blanket. I squeezed his hands and stepped back toward my car. We shared one more lingering glance before we climbed into our respective vehicles and headed out for the day.

The drive to the Bizzy Bean was slow. The early-morning rush had begun, and cars streamed toward the dock to catch the ferry into Mukilteo for their commutes to work. Normally, I would be on my way to work as well, but during my most recent investigation, I had cleared my schedule of any pressing home inspections and had a few more days until I needed to be someplace at a specific time. I parked two blocks from the Bizzy Bean and made my way over for the coven meeting.

Once inside, it was a bit of a madhouse. The line stretched to the front door. Behind the plexiglass enclosure, kittens romped around the space, chasing each other with exuberance. Heather stood behind the counter, calling out orders to Becca and her friend Vicky, who was visiting for the summer. Vicky would be starting at Western Washington

University up in Bellingham next week. I suspected she would come down here regularly, since Becca was one of the few people she was truly close to.

I caught Heather's eye. She nodded and stepped back from the counter, handing off her order-taking duties to Becca, then she ducked under the counter. She followed me into the cat enclosure. Once we were inside, the kittens somehow became even more rambunctious. They hurled themselves around the space, jumping from table to chair and zipping around under the customers' feet. Even with the stress of Meredith's escape, it was hard not to smile at their antics. I tried to cling to that happy feeling as I walked toward the booth at the back, where the rest of my coven, plus my mother and Izzy, were already waiting. Kimberly was nowhere in sight. She had messaged the group that morning saying that she had to drop off her kids at school and to start without her.

I pulled up a chair as Heather claimed the last spot at the end of the booth. Agnes already had the salt ready in her hand. She tossed it into the air as she murmured the words to the spell that would prevent eavesdropping. While any of us could cast it, her specialty in illusions made it stronger than the rest of us could.

The air shimmered with her teal-and-purple haze as the spell settled over the table. I leaned forward, resting my elbows against the table, and updated everyone. Bob was still MIA. The witness was comatose. And we were no closer to figuring out who had killed Jennifer Moore than we had been the evening before. With each word, the women's shoulders around me slumped farther until everyone was almost listless in their seats.

"Now what?" Sarah asked.

I forced myself to sit up straight in my seat. Projecting an image of confidence sometimes helped more than actually feeling confident. I needed my coven to believe that we could do this, because if they didn't believe, then we really couldn't. Magic relied so strongly on our wills that they needed to be as strong as possible if we wanted to prevail. I lifted my hand and ticked off what we had to do. "We have to find Bob, figure out who killed Jennifer Moore, and prepare for the ritual."

Heather nodded along. "And confirm the other descendants are safe."

I swallowed and pushed aside the tightness in my chest as I raised another finger on my hand. "And confirm the other descendants are safe." *How am I supposed to do all that? This is too much. Focus. What will have the biggest impact? Jennifer. Who killed her?* I pursed my lips as I thought over the problem. The Outsider had preyed on Julie's desire for vengeance. "We assumed the Outsider would be using another dead body. But the cemeteries were a dead end. What if… what if the dead body in question isn't in the papers?"

"We could check more cemeteries?" Agnes asked.

I picked at my cuticles. "Maybe. But vengeance is part of it. And vengeance is sensational. If it was a death, or at least a death people know about, it would be in the news, wouldn't it? What if it's a death the newspapers don't know about?"

Megan leaned forward. "Like what?"

My mind worked through the problem. I could feel it at the tip of my tongue, so I continued talking, hoping that the idea would spring out of my mouth. "Someone could have hidden the body, which means the victim, the… now perpetrator, would be a missing person. Maybe what we need to be looking for is missing people."

Betty pulled out her phone. "Then let's make a list and try to find them."

My heart clenched. It was still too much. It was all moving so slowly. *We're going to miss our opportunity.* "We can make the list together. I'll try to find them, and you guys can tackle the rest, maybe? Shoot. We still need to figure out if the other descendants left town."

"I know some magic that can locate people," Lori said.

I tapped my fingers on the table. "I know tracking—"

"It's slower than a typical tracking spell. It doesn't give live updates. But it's more hands off, so it would free us up to do other things." Lori raised her notebook. "It just requires a ghost."

"Sounds like a good idea, but where are we going to find ghosts to do it?" Sarah asked.

I glanced at Izzy. Her shoulders were still hunched, her arms wrapped around herself. She flinched and ducked her head to the side. "Izzy?"

Izzy peered up at me through her curtain of hair. Her tongue darted out to wet her lips. "Yes?"

"How many ghosts are in here right now?"

She grimaced. "Three. The two from the graveyard last night, and I picked up another one this morning."

"Three?" I raised my eyebrows. That was more than I'd expected.

"I'll go to the shelter when I'm done here. I haven't forgotten about Mr. Pickles. I've been busy," Izzy hissed.

Lori rubbed her hands together, a smile spreading across her face. She looked unhinged and almost joyful at the prospect of casting the spell. "Who do we need to find?"

"Let's start with the descendants, Kevin, Jay, and Bob." I jotted down the full names and passed a piece of paper to my mother. If it would send away the ghosts, at least Izzy could focus on the rest of the meeting.

"As you wish." Lori flipped the notebook open and thumbed through the pages to the right one. She leaned over the table and murmured the words to the spell.

Motes of light darted from her mouth. They looked almost exactly like mine, except while mine were gold, hers were a brilliant silver. They had smooth edges and sparkled.

They swirled through the air and split into three streams that stopped a few feet from us. My gaze darted between her and the streams of light. They must have stopped at the ghosts.

After her almost-gleeful expression, I expected to feel *something*. She'd cast a necromantic spell, but the last time I'd been around it, I'd felt wrong. This time, there was no pressure at the back of my head, no warning signs. My magic felt almost calm as she continued to mutter. I bit my lip, studying her. *Why is she so excited?* My heart clenched. I didn't understand her well enough to be sure. I didn't know my mother. And now, part of me wanted to.

I pushed that thought aside and focused on the list. The ghosts would handle the first and last item on the list. We just needed to focus on the next two.

The stream of lights stopped, and Lori settled back into her seat, a sheen of sweat on her forehead. She grabbed a cookie from a plate in the middle and munched on it with her eyes closed. The rest of us exchanged a quick glance then pulled out our phones to begin the task of creating a list of missing persons. One step at a time, we would get it all done.

CHAPTER 8

I leaned back in my chair and stretched my hands over my head to relieve the tension in my shoulders. I had spent the last hour hunched over my phone as the coven worked on making a list of missing persons that could fit the bill. Kim had arrived twenty minutes in and joined in on the missing-person research. A distressing number of people had gone missing in the Seattle area over the last year, just over two hundred. We opted to narrow it down to people who had gone missing on the island within the last six months. That was a much smaller number. We were left with four names that were still listed as missing online, the most promising of which was a woman by the name of Kelsey Harmon. She had gone missing two days before Meredith escaped.

"Did you find anyone else?" I asked.

Heather had to head back to work a few minutes into the search, when a flood of customers came through the door. That left the Retirees, Lori, Izzy, Kim, Megan, and me to search. Grace was back at the house, trying to decompress from all the strong emotions that had surrounded her for the past few days. I mentally checked in with my familiar, Charlie, to make sure things were still going well at the house. I had left him there to keep an eye on her while I was out. He sent back calming emotions. In my experience, over the past few months we had been connected like that, that satisfied feeling only came from one thing: dozing in a sunspot. He was safe. Grace was safe. For the time being.

The Retirees shook their heads, and Megan and Izzy both muttered no's under their breath. My mother didn't respond. She stared out at the cafe, her eyes glazed like she didn't see any of us. I pinched the bridge of my nose. I recognized the expression. She wore it when she was about to take off on one of her grand adventures. I was honestly surprised she hadn't left yet. But the look in her eyes was a reminder that her continued presence at the table wasn't a guarantee. She could wander off at any moment, disappearing for another twenty years.

Lori blinked and cocked her head. Next to her, Izzy sat straighter, her eyes narrowing at a spot over my shoulder.

I looked behind me. "What is it?"

"Bellamy's back," Izzy said.

I blinked, my mind sorting through the names. *Is Bellamy the one with the cat? Why's he back so soon?*

Izzy frowned, and Lori groaned.

"What is it?" I asked.

Izzy crossed her arms. "Kevin Reynolds didn't leave town. He's at his office."

With those words, the pressure at the back of my skull came back. I slumped forward in my seat and hit my head against the counter. I had hoped that the descendants would leave town without an issue. But it couldn't be that simple. It was almost like the world was trying to work against us. I sighed. "I'll go talk to him."

"Are you sure?" Sarah asked.

I pushed myself to my feet and shrugged. "We've met a few times. I'm hoping I'll have more luck convincing him he's in trouble than Chris did. In the meantime, if you guys could finalize the list and begin ritual prep, that would be great."

"I'll put together a dossier based on what I can find online. I'll send you whatever leads I find on Kelsey then work backwards from there." Izzy hunched back over her phone, her fingers flying over the small screen.

I trudged from the cafe. As I walked to my car, I pulled up the directions to Kevin's office. I had only been there one time before, but I still had the address saved. I grumbled under my breath as I drove out of Point Pleasant and headed up the coast to Langley, my head pulsing the entire way. It was midmorning by the time I parked across the street from his small downtown office. It was tucked down an alleyway, with only a small wooden sign, the words Reynold's Family Law pointing the way.

I ducked down the alley and pushed the door open. The space hadn't changed since I'd last been there. A few comfortable-looking chairs lined one wall. A big wooden desk with a woman sitting at it took up the center of the room. The woman's graying hair was pulled into a neat bun at the back of her neck. She peered up at me out of her thick-rimmed glasses.

I glanced at the door behind her. "Is Kevin in?"

"Yes, he's—"

I didn't wait for her to finish. The pressure at the back of my head throbbed, making it difficult to focus on anything but putting one foot in front of the other. With everything going on, it was hard to tell what my divination powers were trying to get me to do. It felt like they were egging me forward, telling me to get into the room now, before something bad happened. Either that or something bad was happening somewhere else, and it was trying to tell me to leave now to fix it. I sighed. *If only it were clearer.* I rounded her desk and pushed open his door.

Kevin sat behind his desk. He froze halfway between

standing and sitting as he stared at me, his mouth agape. He wore his standard rumpled suit, his mousy-brown hair tousled around his head.

"Did you hear from Chris last night?"

Kevin finished sitting. "I did."

I pulled the door closed behind me, cutting off his secretary's objections. "Then what are you still doing in town? I thought you of all people would have heeded his warning—especially after that guy broke into your house."

Kevin held still in his chair, his back straight as he met my gaze. His expression softened, and he offered me a small smile. It warmed his face. "I'm sorry I haven't thanked you properly for saving me that night. I told myself I should call, but to be honest, I wasn't sure what to say. I tried to pass along my gratitude to Chris yesterday, but he didn't stay on the phone long enough to really accept it."

I crossed the room and took the seat across from him. I reached out, pressing my palm into the wood of his desk. "You're in danger, Kevin. I'm… I know we don't know each other well, but I'm worried about you." I poured as much sincerity into my words as I could. *He has to understand. He has to leave.*

"I know." He sighed. "Chris told me someone out there has a grudge against my family line."

"Then you understand why you need to lie low for a couple of days."

He shook his head and looked down at a photo at the edge of his desk. "Maybe. If the line ended with me. But it doesn't."

My gaze flicked between him and the photo. I picked it up. It was of a man, maybe twenty years old, with sandy-blond hair and a pit bull smile from ear to ear. I peered at the man's face. He had Kevin's same kind eyes. I hadn't noticed at first because of a scar bisecting his eyebrow. It gave him an almost roguish look, which was so different from the man across from me.

“What’s his name?”

“Noah.”

I put down the photo. “Why don’t you take him with you?”

Kevin slumped in his seat, his head sliding back. He stared at the ceiling. “If it were only that simple.”

I pushed the photo toward him. “Why don’t you explain it to me?”

“I had a daughter. She was a few years older than him. She had just turned twenty-two. She died in a car accident. My wife—ex-wife now—and I… things fell apart. Noah didn’t take the divorce well. He took her side, even though she’s the one who left. Calling him up and asking him to leave town isn’t an option. He wouldn’t want to hear from me.”

I fought the urge to open my mouth and push. Something about the way he fidgeted in his seat made me think he was more likely to continue if I stayed quiet than if I pushed the issue. I held still until he opened his mouth again.

“I’m not stupid, though. I know we both need to leave town, so I called for backup. His best friend’s coming to help.”

The pressure in my head spiked at the words “best friend.” I gasped and lurched forward, blinking dark spots from my vision.

Kevin sat up. “Are you okay?”

“Who’s his best friend?” I gripped the edge of the desk.

“An old family friend. They grew up together. His name’s Jay.”

My head jerked up. “Jay Mitchell?”

He blinked. “How’d you know?”

My heart raced. “Jay Mitchell is coming to town instead of leaving it?”

Kevin shook his head. "He wouldn't leave without Noah. We're planning on talking to him tonight."

My head pounded. I gritted my teeth against the pain. "It can't wait until tonight. You both need to leave."

"What else do you know?" Kevin stood.

"Please," I pleaded with him.

"I can't just leave without my son."

I floundered. "Can you move up the meeting?"

"I don't know. Probably not, not without ruining my chance of him saying yes. Honestly, I'm not sure if he will. My son… he's willful. He won't want to go too far in case one of his clients needs him. He works as a grief counselor, and he takes his job very seriously."

I collapsed into my seat. *What else can I do? How can I keep them safe if they won't go anywhere?* I closed my eyes and ran through the possibilities. I had assumed that if they left Whidbey Island, it would keep Meredith at bay for a time while she focused on targets closer to home—me, the rest of the coven. *But how are we keeping ourselves safe?* I chewed on my lip. *Wards. That's how.* My head jerked up, and I stared at him. "Would you guys at least agree to come and stay with me and Chris for a few days? Just so we can make sure you're all safe."

Kevin nodded.

I stood and grabbed a pad of paper from his desk. I wrote down my address and slid it toward him.

Kevin picked up the pad of paper and ripped off the page. "If all goes well, we'll be there before dinner."

The pressure in my head receded. I sagged in my chair. It wasn't gone yet, but something had just been diverted. I sighed and stood. "Thank you."

My shoulders were still tense as I strode out of his office. His secretary glared at me as I slipped past her desk. I marched back to my car, my fingers tapping on my leg as I moved. One disaster averted, but my to-do list wasn't any shorter. I texted my coven, updating them on the situation.

> **MEGAN:**
> I'll ask Kim if she can pop by your place to add more wards, just in case.

> **SARAH:**
> The rest of us are working with Lori on ritual prep. We need to go through a ton of steps if we want to do it tomorrow. Call if you need anything.

> **DANI:**
> Thanks. Going to try to track down the first missing person on our list.

I exited the chat and pulled up the information Izzy had sent me while I was in my meeting with Kevin. It was a series of photos of Kelsey Harmon, the missing woman, with the last one being a close-up of a tattoo.

> **IZZY:**
> I couldn't find any commonly worn items. This is the closest I could get.

I climbed into my car and stared at the photo. *Will a tracking spell even work on a tattoo?* Only one way to find out.

CHAPTER 9

I drummed my fingers against the steering wheel. I hadn't put the car into drive yet as the tracking spell rattled around in my head. Something was off. I felt certain I could find her. But I was also just as certain that the tracking spell as I knew it wouldn't work. I turned the problem over in my mind, whispering the words to the spell under my breath. I continued to tap my fingers against the steering wheel and replayed the words in my head. The tracking spell was too focused on the thing I was seeking being an item. While my intent was to find a person, the words and intent would be misaligned. It would require too much focus to maintain.

I pulled out my notebook and jotted down the two tracking spells I knew. The first one could find something on a map, and the second could lay out a trail in front of me. Both focused on an object. I tapped the pen against the page. A person's identity shifted with their mood, their surroundings, their day. People weren't static enough. The tattoo was. But it wasn't an object. I jotted my thoughts in the margins and played with the wording. I had never modified a spell on my own, but as I scribbled, something felt right about it. I knew the theories. And tracking spells had somehow turned into my specialty. I rewrote the spell a few different ways until the words flowed correctly on the page. I stared down at it, reading it two more times before I nodded and flipped to the next page to begin drawing.

It was a simple tattoo, a word: Elsbeth. The name was on her wrist, with a small, delicate flower at the end. The tattoo was black and white, no color. While I wasn't as skilled as my daughter, I was good enough that I could copy the style. I drew the image on a piece of paper and held it out in front of me. *Am I being arrogant? I'm still a baby witch. Am I ready to be writing my own spells?* I exhaled sharply out of my mouth and cracked my neck. *What's the worst that could happen? It doesn't work, and I call for help? I can do this.*

I shook out my arms and stared at the drawing as I murmured the words to the spell I'd written. Golden motes of light flowed from my mouth toward the drawing. From there, they began to float away from me down the street, making a trail for me to follow. Before they got too far, I used a trick I had learned from Kim and reached out to grab the light. I steadied my breathing as I continued to murmur, my fingers rolling the light together.

Sweat gathered on my forehead as I pushed forward. *Am I trying too many things at once? Please work. It will work.* I repeated those words in my head as I continued to spin the motes of light into a thread. Once I had a few feet of thread to work with, I folded the piece of paper into a small square and tied the golden thread around it. I willed it to attach to the drawing and to continue the path forward. My fingers shook as I tied the last knot, and something clicked into place. My words cut off. I held my breath, staring at the small stream of light that flowed away from my car toward something. The light held.

I slumped into my seat and grabbed a protein bar from my purse. I inhaled the bar in a few bites then grabbed another. Magic like that was draining. But it seemed to be working. I set the piece of paper on the phone mount on my dashboard then shoved my phone against it to lock everything in place. Confident it wouldn't go away, I switched my car into drive and pulled away from the curb.

My gaze flicked between the roadway in front of me and the string of golden light that disappeared down the street. I followed it through Langley and headed farther north, up the coast to Oak Harbor. The line led inland to a series of single-story buildings that were part of an apartment complex. I slowly drove through the lot and stared at the building it disappeared into. It didn't look any different than the other units. The nondescript gray walls had an equally bland tan metal roof. The yards were neat, and the cars remaining in the parking lot were older models but well maintained. I parked and stared at the door.

Getting out of the car, I walked around the building, comparing the unit the line disappeared into to the neighbors'. There was no welcome mat, and the blinds were drawn. It almost looked vacant. Almost. If I hadn't been staring straight at the window, I might have missed the movement. Someone was staring at me from between the blinds. They hadn't opened them far. If not for the fact that they had swayed when someone touched them, I wouldn't have noticed. I cocked my head and stared at the window.

It was an odd sensation. I could feel someone's eyes on me. But it wasn't a dangerous feeling. The hair on my arms didn't rise. The pressure at the back of my skull had remained a dull ache—no pulsing, just a sensation in my chest that I associated with being watched. I took a faltering step toward the door and paused. *Why are they watching me?* I tapped my fingers against my leg and stepped back. I relaxed my eyes and brought my magic to the surface so I could look at the building. There were no signs of a spell, no lingering goo like what the Outsider had left behind at prior crime scenes. The only thing out of place was the feeling in my chest.

The door cracked open. "Did he send you?" A woman's voice came through the narrow space.

I blinked and took a step forward to see who was speaking. Through the sliver, all I could see of the woman was a hazel eye, wide and fearful.

I swallowed and softened my voice to appear nonthreatening. "I'm not sure who you're talking about. No one sent me."

The door opened another half inch, revealing a little more of the woman behind it—Kelsey Harmon, the woman I was there to find. She was dressed in an oversized T-shirt and baggy pants that hid her body.

She peered at me from over the chain. "Why are you here?"

I opened my mouth and closed it. I didn't have a good reason, not one she would understand.

"Are you here looking for me?" Her voice broke on the word *me*.

I studied her. Her shoulders were squared, like she was ready to fight or flee. A faint bruise covered her jaw. *Ooooh.* I recognized the look in her eye. It reminded me of Becca after she first escaped from Cyrus. Kelsey wasn't missing. She was running from someone.

"I was, but it's not what you think."

"Do I have to run?" she asked.

"No." I shook my head.

"Are you sure? I… I spent all my money to rent this place. I can't afford to run, but I will if I have to. So please, please be honest with me. Do I have to run?" Her words came out fast but strong.

I don't have time for this, but I can't leave her scared. What should I do? I shook my head again and pulled out a notebook from my pocket. "I'm here to help."

"What?"

I quickly jotted down two names and numbers. Abby and her father, Keith Sinclair, had promised to do me a favor someday after I helped clear her name when circumstances outside her control had put her in Bob's crosshairs as the prime suspect in a murder investigation. They both had experience in starting over. If anyone could help Kelsey, they could. I ripped the piece of paper from my notebook and inched forward until it was within easy reach. "I have friends who can help you. Tell them Dani told you to call."

Kelsey accepted the slip of paper and stared at it. "Is this legit?"

I nodded and held her gaze.

She studied my face, her expression slowly softening. She folded the piece of paper and held it to her chest. "Thank you."

I took a step back then turned and trudged back to my car. I pulled out my phone and texted Abby.

DANI:
If someone named Kelsey reaches out to you, could you consider that me calling in my favor?

ABBY:
Of course. Who's Kelsey?

DANI:
A woman fleeing a bad situation.

ABBY:
Consider it done. And no favor needed.

DANI:
You sure?

ABBY:
Use it on something selfish. Helping Kelsey would just be me paying it forward for all the help I received back in the day.

I collapsed into the front seat of my car. I closed my eyes to mentally check in on Charlie again. He was a little less content this time. He wasn't pleased about so many people being at the house. They weren't petting him. How rude.

I bit my lip as I pulled up my other missed messages on my phone. Izzy had sent me a dossier on the next missing person. Raymond Ellison was a dentist and had been missing for a day. I scrolled through the photos she'd sent me. The only item he always wore was a wedding ring. I zoomed in on it and grabbed another protein bar from my purse. I chewed on the bar as I sketched out the next drawing. My new tracking spell had worked better than expected, and I wanted to give it another go. I was halfway through my snack when my phone rang, Chris's name flashing across the screen.

"Hey, babe, what's up?" I asked.

"I have a lead on Bob, but I'll need your help." Chris sounded tired, the stress of the day wearing on him.

I stared down at the drawing. "What do you need me to do?"

"Meet me at O'Malley's."

My jaw dropped. O'Malley's was a dive bar. *What on earth is he doing there?* I cleared my throat. Chris didn't need me to question why Bob was at a bar. His mentor was hurting. Besides, there was no guarantee that Raymond would be the body the Outsider had possessed. If he wasn't and Bob died while I was chasing down a bad lead, I would never forgive myself. Chris's despair wouldn't let me. Finding Bob was more important than finding Raymond. With tomorrow being the first night of the full moon, if we could keep the descendants safe through the night, it wouldn't matter who the Outsider was using anymore. The curse would be broken. Meredith would be resting. And the Outsider would be able to go home.

I sighed. "I'll be there in forty minutes."

CHAPTER 10

It took me longer to get to O'Malley's than I would have liked. I hit traffic when I reached downtown as people got off work for the day and everyone tried to go home at the same time. I pulled into the parking lot almost an hour later and claimed a spot next to Chris. He stood leaning against his car, his arms crossed over his broad chest. He stepped away from the vehicle, his hand running over his head as he approached me. His hair stood at awkward angles, as if he had run his fingers through his short-cropped hair many times. Sighing, he wrapped his arms around me, dropping his head onto my shoulder.

I wrapped my arms around him. "Are you okay?"

"Collecting Bob has proven difficult. I didn't want to call you, but my first attempt to convince him to leave the bar failed spectacularly. I knew I needed backup. If he gets riled up like that again, I'll have to arrest the guy, and he would never forgive me for that."

I pulled back and studied his face, quirking my eyebrow at him. "You do remember that he isn't my biggest fan, right?"

Chris nodded. "And if all goes according to plan, he won't

see you right away. I was kind of hoping you could use your calming mojo on him."

I pressed my lips together. I still hadn't experimented much with alcohol and calming potions. The one and only time I'd used it, the potion had seemed to increase alcohol's tendency to remove inhibitions. And that guy had been a happy drunk.

I wasn't sure how it would work with Bob, but I was willing to give it a shot if it helped Chris. "All right. Let's do this."

Chris took the lead, pushing open the bar's front door. He stuck his head in first then motioned for me to follow. I ducked in behind him and sidled along the back wall as I waited for my eyes to adjust. Outside, the sun was bright, but inside, with all the windows covered by posters, it was dim. My gaze swept along the bar on the far wall. Only a few patrons occupied the stools. To the right was a group of three, and all the way at the end of the bar, as far from everyone else as he could get, was Bob. He sat hunched forward, his head hung low as he sipped at a glass of amber liquid. His hair had grown out since I'd last seen him, the salt-and-pepper locks shaggy as they brushed the tops of his ears. His shirt was rumpled and stained. Even from here, I could feel the hollowness. He was beyond caring. He was nothing.

Bob had never been nothing before. My mouth went dry. I licked my lips to wet them and exhaled slowly. I held my gaze on Bob and murmured the words to the relaxation potion. Golden motes of light zipped across the room and floated around his drink before sinking into the liquid. It was at times like this that I was glad only witches could see magic. I stared as Bob raised his glass to his lips again and took another sip. I held my breath, waiting for the lights swirling around the glass to seep into his skin. It was subtle.

The warm glow slowly flowed from his head throughout his body.

Once it hit his feet, I exhaled and pushed Chris forward. "Go now while the spell's still holding."

Chris marched across the room and dropped down on the stool next to Bob. He leaned over and began talking. From my position, I couldn't hear what he said. I could just see his lips moving. My gaze flicked between them, studying their body language. Bob flinched slightly when Chris sat down, but he was relaxed again, his shoulders loose. For a second, a ghost of a smile crossed his lips.

Chris stood and put his hand on Bob's shoulder. "Come back with me so you can sleep it off."

Bob lumbered to his feet. I darted away from my spot against the wall and scampered toward the front door before he could turn all the way around and see me. I sprinted toward my car and threw myself behind the wheel as Bob stumbled out of the bar, his arm wrapped loosely around Chris's shoulders.

Great. Not just Bob at my house but a drunk Bob at that. I grimaced. A drunk Bob was still better than a dead Bob. While I didn't like the guy, no one deserved to be killed for something their father did.

I waited until Bob was slumped inside Chris's car, his head resting against the window, before I started my engine. I inched out of my spot and exited the parking lot ahead of Chris. As I drove through town back to my house, I periodically glanced into my rear-view mirror. Chris was half a block behind me the entire way.

It's just one night. Right? Tomorrow's the full moon. It's just one night, maybe two. I can handle Bob for a night or two.

My jaw dropped when I pulled into my driveway and saw past the tree line for the first time. Every spot in front of my house had been claimed. Lori's truck was still there as well as

Grace's small hatchback. Behind that were three cars I didn't recognize. I drove up onto the grass and parked.

Is it a good idea to have them all in one place? I shook my head, banishing the thought before it had a chance to make me more anxious, then exited my car. I trudged toward my front door, my hands shoved deep into my pockets to keep them steady.

I opened my front door and was greeted by a cacophony of sounds. Music blared from the stereo in the living room. Grace laughed in the kitchen. A guy's laugh followed a second later. I cocked my head and inched forward. I hadn't heard Grace laugh in months. I couldn't remember the last time I had heard such a carefree sound from her. I peered around the corner.

Seated at the kitchen table was Kevin with a laptop in front of him. He wore headphones, blocking out the noise. On the table next to him sat Charlie, half asleep with his front paws covering his face. Farther into the kitchen stood Grace, a stirring spoon coated with tomato sauce in her gloved hand, her dark-brown eyes wide with delight. Next to her, leaning back against the counter, was a guy I had never seen in person before. I recognized him from the photo on Kevin's desk. His sandy-blond hair hung low over his forehead, half covering his eyes. He grinned widely as he talked with his hands. And next to him was a guy I hadn't seen in almost a year, Jay Mitchell. He still had the same charming smile and golden-brown hair. He was doubled over, his hand half covering his mouth as he struggled to breathe past the laughter.

"You didn't!" Grace took half a step toward Kevin's son, Noah.

He raised his hands in front of him, shrugging as his smile grew wider. "All I'm saying is he deserved it."

I glanced between the trio as I took another small step

forward. The floorboards creaked under me, and Grace's head jerked in my direction.

Her smile froze for half a second before it softened at my approach. "Hey, Mom. Have you met our new houseguests yet?"

Jay straightened. His smile shifted from joy filled to friendly. "I've got to be honest, I didn't expect to see you again. Though, if what Deputy Harris says is true, I'm not surprised. My life as I know it is in danger. And here you are to rescue me again, like my personal guardian angel."

I gaped at him. *What—guardian angel?* I blinked and took a step into the room. "I'm just doing what anyone would in a similar position. Helping."

Jay's small smile widened into a grin, and he laughed. He wiped at his eyes. "You're joking, right?"

My gaze swiveled from Jay to Grace to Kevin's son. They all stared at me like I had grown a second head. *Am I missing something?* I forced a smile. "No? I mean, maybe not everyone. But most people try to do the right thing when they can."

Noah shook his head. "Not if it inconveniences them." He glanced at Grace, his expression softening. "And from what I can tell, the apple didn't fall far from the tree. I really appreciate how welcoming you both have been."

The living room door clattered closed behind me. I turned toward the sound.

Bob stumbled forward, his face red. "What are you doing here?"

I stared at him, my mind whirling. I opened my mouth to respond, but when I stared at him straight on, his eyes weren't pointed at me. I followed his line of sight. He was staring at Jay. My gaze bounced between them. Jay straightened, his eyes narrowing.

What is going on? I've missed something. I opened my mouth to speak but stopped when Chris grabbed Bob by the shoulder and tugged him into the living room.

"I'll go make up the guest rooms." Grace dropped the spoon into the saucepan and moved toward me, all the color draining from her face. "Mom, do you mind taking over the cooking?"

She shuffled toward the hallway. Charlie hopped off the table and sauntered down the hall after her. I stood frozen for a second before following her down the hall. I replayed happy memories as I approached to even out my mood.

"Are you okay, sweetheart?" I asked.

Grace leaned back against the wall and closed her eyes. "It just got heavy in there all of a sudden. I'm working through the emotional whiplash."

"Can I do anything to help?" I asked.

Grace straightened. "Leave Charlie with me? He's always good at calming things down."

I had opened my mouth to respond when Noah walked into the hallway next to me. "Mind if I help prep the rooms too?" He stopped in front of me and held out his hand. "I'm Noah, by the way. Nice to meet you officially."

Grace looked at him, a small smile coming back to her lips. She was much too empathetic to be around Bob right now. But somehow, this Noah kid was fine. I studied him for a second. I wasn't as good at reading people as Grace. While she could pick things up in the air, I usually had to touch something to tell what emotions someone had felt—unless it was a particularly strong one. I took his hand in both of mine, my fingers touching the corner of his long-sleeved shirt, and smiled. His emotions through the shirt were quiet somehow. I could feel them, but his base state was calm with a touch of amusement.

"It's nice to meet you too." I released his hand and stepped back. "I should get back to the cooking before the water boils over."

Grace nodded and turned to Noah. "You can help, but

only because I need someone on Charlie duty. He's a menace when I'm trying to make a bed."

They disappeared down the hallway. I returned to the kitchen, my gaze bouncing from person to person. Jay stood stock-still in the middle of the room, his hands clenched at his sides. Chris was with Bob in the living room, his hand on his mentor's shoulder and his head bowed toward Bob as he murmured something in a conciliatory tone. Kevin still sat at the kitchen table with his headphones on. His shoulders appeared tenser than when I'd entered. He wasn't blind to everything going on. He just was opting not to get involved. I sighed and walked to the stove, taking a quick inventory of everything. French bread had been cut open and lay on the counter. Garlic butter sat in a bowl. The oven was preheated. And on the stove, a pot of noodles boiled beside a pan of meat sauce.

"Need any help?" Jay asked.

"Sure." I picked up the garlic butter. "Could you prep the garlic bread? It looks like that needs to go in next."

Jay wordlessly spread the garlic butter as I stirred the sauce.

"What's he doing here?" Bob asked again, his voice tense.

"Let's get some food into you—" Chris began.

"No. Answer the question," Bob demanded.

My fingers twitched on the spoon as my heart rate climbed, pounding in my ears. *What on earth?* Rage. I swallowed it down, trying to control it. Bob was spewing his emotions into the air. I battled against them, trying to cling to my own and not succumb to his. While Noah had been emotionally quiet, Bob was like a thunderstorm.

"Why is *he* here?" Bob hissed.

"Because you're both on the list!" I spun, spittle forming at the corner of my mouth.

Bob's eyes widened, and he surged to his feet. He glared at me, fists clenching and unclenching at his sides, then he turned and stomped away. He slammed the front door open and disappeared outside.

Chris charged after him. "Bob, wait!"

The second he was gone, the tension in my shoulders dissipated. My heart rate plummeted until it was back to normal. I sagged against the counter.

"Are you okay?" Jay whispered.

I shook my head. "And I thought he hated me. What's he got against you?"

Jay shrugged. "My attorney may have been a tad aggressive when the sheriff tried to arrest me for my dad's murder."

"He probably deserved it," I murmured.

Jay snorted. "He did."

We finished preparing dinner in silence. As Jay pulled the garlic bread from the broiler, I drained the pasta and mixed it in with the sauce. We moved around each other as we quickly prepped the plates. Grace and Noah slipped back into the room and claimed adjoining seats at the table. Kevin closed his laptop as I dropped the prepared garlic bread in front of him. Jay carried the plates of food and deposited them in front of everyone before taking a seat against the far wall. He picked up his fork to take a bite as Bob and Chris stepped back into the room.

Bob stared at the floor as he shuffled to the table and collapsed into a seat. Chris claimed the spot next to me, shooting me an apologetic smile. I grabbed one more plate from the cupboard and dished out a serving for Bob, sliding it in front of him before I flopped into my chair.

"So… are we going to address the elephant in the room?" Jay asked.

Everyone at the table tensed. I gripped my fork, mentally preparing myself to survive another explosion from Bob.

Jay looked around. "Why are our names on a hit list?"

I sagged.

Chris shifted in his seat. "It's still under investigation. We don't fully understand it yet. But in an abundance of caution—"

"Codswallop," Bob grumbled.

"What?" I asked.

Bob leaned forward and pointed his fork at Jay. "It's because we're both descended from bad men. And karma doesn't care. It doesn't care because the sins of the father roll downhill anyway."

"That's one hell of a mixed metaphor," Noah said.

Bob slumped into his chair and pulled out a flask.

"Bob—" Chris reached for it.

Bob shrugged him off, surged to his feet, and stumbled toward the living room. "I'm taking the couch."

I gritted my teeth. *Just one day,* I reminded myself. *A living Bob is better than a dead one. Just one day. Maybe two.*

Noah inched forward in his seat and lowered his voice. "How long do we have to stay here with that grump?" He cocked his head toward the living room.

"A day or so, assuming things go well," I said, echoing my thoughts from a moment before.

"If things go well?" Kevin asked.

"Yep. Not long at all if things go well." *I hope. If we don't break the curse over the three days of the full moon, we'll have to wait until next month. Can I keep them safe that long?* "We'll know more soon. I promise."

We sat in silence for almost a full minute as we all stared down at our plates. They were all scared. I could feel the tingles of it at the back of my mind.

"This is really good." Kevin pointed to his food. "Thanks so much for cooking."

I blinked up at him. It was like he had made the decision to make this seem as normal as he could—just friends enjoying a home-cooked meal, no killer on the loose, no angry drunk in the other room.

I smiled weakly at him and accepted the invitation to ignore the stress while we ate dinner. "Anytime."

I only half listened as the people around the table started to talk. *I can keep them safe for tonight. But how much longer? I have to find the Outsider. I have to break this curse. I... No,* we *have to. Stop trying to do it all on your own.* I exhaled slowly through my mouth. *We have to. I have a coven. It isn't all on me. We have to.* I pushed my pasta around my plate with my fork. *Tomorrow, I'll hit the ground running to find whatever body the Outsider is using. I'll search for Raymond. My coven will handle the rest. We've got this. We just need to survive the night with Bob.*

CHAPTER 11

I paused at the top of the stairs. The early-morning light streamed in through the windows. From the living room, Bob's snores echoed through the house like a chain saw. I clasped my shoes in one hand as I tiptoed down the stairs. While it was my house, something about waking guests ratcheted up my anxiety. I slipped into the kitchen, set my shoes by the door, and slinked across the room. The warm but bitter scent of coffee filled the air. I had thought ahead and prepped it before going to bed, setting the timer to begin brewing a few minutes before seven o'clock. I poured a generous amount of creamer into a mug and topped it with coffee. With my morning pick-me-up in hand, I settled on a stool at the kitchen counter and pulled my bag toward me from its usual place. I fished out a notepad and opened a picture of the missing dentist on my phone.

Izzy had sent me five different pictures of him with the ring circled. It was the only thing he seemed to always have on him. I zoomed in on the ring so I wouldn't have to look at his face. I didn't know what I would find when I went looking for him. Part of me hoped he was off on a fishing trip and had forgotten to tell his wife where he was going. I doubted it, though. His expression held a gentleness. His eyes were kind, and the neatly trimmed beard reminded me of my grandfather. I chewed on my lip as I drew the ring.

Floorboards creaked behind me. I stiffened as someone stopped a few inches from my back. Then the scent of sandalwood and something uniquely Chris filled my nose, and I relaxed.

He wrapped his arms around me, resting his chin on my shoulder. "What are you working on?" he murmured.

"A focus for a tracking spell. I'm going to try finding the next missing person on our list."

He nodded, his chin lightly digging into my shoulder. "I'll walk you to your car when you're ready."

I patted his hand resting over my stomach. He squeezed me once then backed away to pour himself a travel mug. I peered at him from the corner of my eye, smothering a smile as he poured an even more generous portion of creamer into his mug.

We drank our coffee in a companionable silence. I was sipping the last of my drink when Charlie slipped into the room and wound his way through my legs, purring up a storm.

I dipped my hand to scratch him behind his tail. "Hey, buddy," I whispered.

He ducked his head under my hand, demanding more pets. Through our bond, he sent me feelings of encouragement with a tinge of longing. He hated staying at the house so many days in a row, but with all the people here, he knew I would want him to keep an eye on things.

"Thank you for being understanding. I really need you here to help Grace. I'm worried about her with so many people in the house." I scratched him behind his ears and stood. Without another word, I grabbed my stuff. I cocked my head toward Chris and walked to the front door, stopping briefly to snag my shoes on the way out.

I slipped my feet into them on the front porch and made my way down to the cars parked on the grass. Chris linked his fingers with mine as we stepped onto the dew-covered ground.

He squeezed my hand. "I've been thinking. We should go for a spring wedding."

I blinked at him.

He smiled, redness creeping up his neck as he blushed. "Too much?"

"No, just surprised it's on your mind. That's all."

He nodded. "Everything is intense right now. I feel like I'll drown in the moment if I don't have something to look forward to."

I wrapped my arm around his waist as we continued our slow walk toward our vehicles. "I like the idea of a spring wedding. I've always thought flower crown veils were beautiful."

Chris hummed in agreement. "Plus, if it's later in the spring, we can have ice cream."

I chuckled and unlocked my car. "So long as it's not the cake."

He squeezed my hand again and left me so he could climb into his own vehicle. I collapsed into the front seat and pulled out the notepad with the ring drawing. The tracking spell I had written the day before worked better than the others I had previously used. I murmured the words to it, the motes of lights swirling forward. I made quick work of forming the light into a string and tying it around the folded piece of paper. Like the day before, I tucked it behind my phone then followed the string of lights with my car.

I pushed thoughts of the wedding aside and focused on the next step. My coven would be up and working on preparing for the ritual soon. I had to rely on them to get it done while I continued working on what I did best—investigating.

The drive through Point Pleasant was slow. Traffic inched forward in the downtown section but eased up once I hit the outskirts. When I entered the part of town that the revitalization project hadn't reached yet, the streets were empty. With the small port in town, a developer had tried to turn Point Pleasant into a shipping hub back in the sixties. It hadn't gone well. With Seattle so close, the region didn't need another one. Instead, a row of warehouses sat empty and abandoned. I frowned as the golden thread of light disappeared into one of the warehouses.

I circled the block. As I drove around the building, the line of light stayed consistent. It continued to flow from the piece of paper on my dashboard into the abandoned building. *What on earth?* I parked and drummed my fingers on my leg. The windows on the ground floor had been boarded up. A chain-link fence surrounded the building, but it sagged in places. The lot was overgrown, with weeds pushing up out of the concrete. It didn't look like anyone had been there in years.

Sighing, I grabbed the piece of paper and approached the building on foot. I slipped through a break in the fence and padded around the structure. No matter what angle I came at it from, the light from my tracking spell disappeared inside. The dentist's ring was in there. *But why?* I studied the building in earnest, looking for a way in. The front door had a large padlock on it, and the back door was more of a fire escape than an entrance. It didn't have a handle to pull on. Chewing on my lip, I let my gaze travel up the structure until I was looking at the windows higher up the sides. One of the windows had been broken in, and enough debris covered the building's side that if I climbed up it, I could probably get inside.

I stretched my shoulders and touched my toes. Gritting my teeth, I lifted myself up onto the stack of broken crates. It shifted under my weight. I paused, waiting to see if it would hold. It did. I grabbed a bit higher on the stack and pulled myself up. Nothing moved as I scaled the side of the building. Perching on the last of the crates, I stood, gripped the window ledge, and hoisted myself up. All those days at the gym had paid off. I hauled myself onto the window ledge and peered inside.

The warehouse interior was dark and musty. Dust motes swirled in the slivers of sunlight that made it through the grime-covered windowpanes. I glanced down at a platform about six feet below the window with stairs a few feet away that led into the belly of the beast. I shifted my weight and lowered myself until I was hanging from my fingertips. At the last second, I wondered if the platform would hold. But it was too late. My fingers slipped.

I dropped with a thud onto the platform. It creaked under me. I threw my arms wide, ready to grab onto something. A plume of dust floated around me. I coughed and waved my hand in front of my face to clear the air. The platform was sturdy under my feet. Tentatively, I took a step forward, then another, until I was scampering down the stairs, following the thin thread of light. As soon as I hit the ground floor, the light dimmed further. Clouds must have moved in outside, obscuring what little light did make it through. While I could still see the thread of light straight ahead of me, it wasn't bright enough to light the area.

Using my phone as a flashlight, I crept forward, following the thread deeper into the abandoned building. It curved forward and stopped at a shape in the middle of the floor at the center of the room. My breath hitched in my throat. The shape was recognizable. It was a person lying on their back in a circle that looked exactly like the one we'd found Jennifer Moore in at Meredith's house. I inched forward until my phone's light illuminated the man's face. I swallowed. I had found Raymond Ellison, and he was dead.

CHAPTER 12

I stumbled back from the body and paced. *How did he get here? Why was he killed?* I steadied my breathing. *How is this connected to Meredith?* I relaxed my eyes and studied the scene as best I could, fighting the rising bile at the back of my throat. I didn't think I would ever get used to seeing dead bodies. The longer I stared at him, the darker the room got. The shadows deepened, and the little spots of light stood out starker against the black. Nothing sparkled, though, and no green goop like the Outsider had left behind before marked the scene—no signs of magic. *He's in a ritual circle. Why aren't there signs of magic? And why is the pressure in my head pulsing?* I inched forward, staring at the ground around him. Dust covered it. It was almost like he had dropped into place in the center of the circle. I craned my head up. He couldn't have fallen from above.

I bit my lip and pulled out my phone to text Chris.

DANI:
I found the dentist. He's dead.

CHRIS:
Are you safe?

DANI:
Yes.

CHRIS:
Where are you?

I texted him the address and pushed the phone back into my pocket then turned toward the stairs. The second my foot hit the first step, the pressure in my head exploded. I backed away, and it simmered down to a slow, steady pulse. I gritted my teeth. At least my divination powers weren't subtle about wanting me to take a closer look. I inched back toward the center of the room, my hand darting out to touch a few of the broken pieces of wood and rusted-out pieces of machinery that littered the floor. My eyes watered as sadness filled me when I brushed a cracked piece of glass. My fingers slid across a few more objects. With each one, they alternated between boredom and despondency. I stopped two feet from the body and brushed the backs of my knuckles across the top of the mostly intact crate that stood closest to Raymond.

Something fluttered in my stomach, and my breath hitched in my throat. A tingle ran through my body as I rocked forward onto the balls of my feet. Anticipation. Ambition. I cocked my head, trying to dissect the feeling rushing through me. *Greed.* I lurched away from the crate and rubbed my hand against my stomach to rid myself of the feeling. I wasn't sure how I knew, but I was certain the emotion was connected to the man in front of me. It was what his killer had felt. It was too new and fresh. All the other emotions had been muted with time. This one, this twisted joy, was how the killer had felt.

I swallowed rapidly, trying to force the bile back down. *This has something to do with how Meredith got out. But how? There's no magic. Maybe it wasn't the Outsider? No. She didn't know anyone else who could or would help. Everyone connected to her is a target. I've... got to figure out who released Meredith.* The pressure in my skull spiked again. I gritted my teeth. *Not now.* The pressure wouldn't go away. Cursing under my breath, I grabbed the small obsidian mirror I kept in my pocket and flipped it open. As soon as my eyes landed on the smooth plane of black glass, the pressure went away.

"Okay. Okay, I get it. I have to look backward. Are you happy?" I grumbled.

I inched toward the body as I murmured the words to the spell that would activate my Sight. It was the only way I knew to force a vision. Golden motes of light flew from my mouth and danced around the room before surging back toward me and sinking into the mirror. With one eye on the glass, I kept the other one trained ahead of me so I could keep track of my surroundings as the mirror pulsed with light then became black.

I frowned, both my eyes moving toward the mirror. The darkness spread across my vision, swallowing me whole. It was cloying as it gripped me. Everything went black, turning to darkness and silence. I couldn't even hear myself breathe. I ripped the mirror away from my face, spun on my heel, and hightailed it up the stairs. My legs pumped under me as I ran toward the window. I jumped up, pushing against the wall, and scrambled until my fingers found the ledge. Relying on my forward momentum, I clambered up into the windowsill. My fight-or-flight instincts blared. I barely registered that I was still moving until I was halfway down the pile of crates at the side of the building, one hand moving after another until my feet landed safely on the ground.

Shuddering, I walked as calmly as I could toward the fence. I slipped back through the gap I had come through earlier and marched across the street to my car. I rested my head against the warm metal and counted back from ten. What I had felt in there disturbed me. Greed. Darkness. *Was it dark when he died, or did that mean something? It had to mean something. It was like the darkness was alive.* With my eyes closed, I replayed in my head the different conversations that had led me here. I chased the line of thought back to the first conversation, the one with my mother before the green light split open the sky.

The darkness is coming.

I jolted upright and pulled out my phone again. I opened my contacts and scrolled until I found my mother's name. *Let's hope she hasn't changed her number.*

DANI:
What can you tell me about the darkness?

I stared at my phone, willing her to answer.

A car pulled up next to me and came to a stop. I glanced over, finding Chris's face behind the wheel. A second car was trailing him, a second cruiser. I sighed and pushed my phone into my pocket.

Chris climbed out of the vehicle and jerked his thumb toward the building behind me. "Is the body in there?"

I nodded.

Harrison unfolded from the second cruiser and strode toward us. I craned my neck to properly see his face. He stood straighter than usual. He normally hunched his back, bending his easily six-foot-five-plus frame into one closer to Chris's height. Today, he towered over us. Standing fully straight, he didn't look as lanky as normal. He still gave the impression of someone who had been stretched. But his shoulders were back, making him seem wider too. He frowned at me, his eyes flicking to the building Chris pointed toward.

"Ma'am, did you call this in?" he asked.

I grimaced and nodded.

He sighed and ran his hand over his face. "Did you miss the No Trespassing sign?"

I glanced between him and the fence. I grimaced again as

I spotted the sign hanging from one corner, attached halfway down the fence. "Um…"

He looked up at the sky. "I'm sure you heard something strange, or… something. But since you're here and I'll have to note you here in my official report, you should probably come into the station to answer a few questions."

Chris opened his mouth, but I held my hand up to stop him. Harrison didn't want to take me in. That much was clear. But if Chris intervened, they could both get in trouble. With Bob's resignation paperwork still back at the station, Chris would have even more eyes on him, watching how he would perform as the acting sheriff. I wasn't about to mess that up for him—no matter how inconvenient it was.

"Of course. I'd be happy to." I forced a smile. "Is it okay if I call my daughter first? She'll worry if I don't come home."

He nodded and stepped aside. He hunched his shoulders, lowering his head to confer with Chris. They spoke in hushed voices about securing the scene and next steps. Chris was giving him directions, while Harrison grumbled that he knew how to take a witness statement. He stressed the word "witness."

I took a few steps away from them and called Megan.

"Hey, Dani." Megan answered on the second ring.

"I found Raymond Ellison. He's dead, in a similar ritual circle as Jennifer Moore. I can't help but feel I'm missing something. Could you ask Lori what she meant about 'the *darkness* is coming'? Was it a literal darkness? A figurative one?"

"So, it's connected?"

My instincts warred with one another. It obviously was, but I didn't know how. *Why would Raymond Ellison be a victim at all?* Unless Meredith's ghost needed fuel or something. *Life has power, right? What if they were both used to power something? But if so, what needed powering?* "I don't know. I think so. Something felt off."

Harrison took a step toward me and gestured to his cruiser. "Follow me in?"

I nodded and turned away to finish my call. "Just ask her. I've got to go give a witness statement."

"Will you be back in time for this evening?" Megan asked.

I swallowed. This was our opportunity to put Meredith to rest and end everything. "I wouldn't miss it for the world."

I hung up and scampered back to my car. Harrison was doing his best, but he really did need to question me because of all the eyes looking at the department right now. I sighed. It was terrible timing. I grumbled under my breath as I followed him to the worn-down double-wides still serving as the temporary sheriff's station at the edge of town. Hopefully, giving a witness statement wouldn't take too long. But knowing my luck, I would be there all day.

CHAPTER 13

The interview with Harrison went longer than I would have liked. We spent most of the afternoon off the record as I answered question after question. At midday, he sent Peggy on a lunch run, and she came back with burgers and shakes from Slice of Life. He kicked her out of the room, and we hunkered down to continue the interview.

It was a strange experience. He frequently didn't take the first answer and instead poked and prodded until something came out that wasn't entirely how things had gone down but that looked good on paper—not just for him but for me as well. He was bending over backwards to ensure there would be no need for a single follow-up question or sidelong glance over me finding another body. At first, it confused me. I spent half the day reading his emotional state through the table. All I could feel from him was trust and a desire to protect. I wasn't sure what I had done to garner those emotions. But I could see how, like Bob was Chris's mentor, Chris had become Harrison's.

As it got closer to dinnertime, we finalized my statement, and I scurried from the sheriff's station. I drove through

Point Pleasant, my grip tight on the steering wheel. I glanced at the sky. The sun was beginning to set. It hung low over the horizon, blanketing the area in warm-orange hues mixed with a deep purple. I kept my foot steady on the gas, trying not to speed too much as I got closer to home. My coven had been prepping all day, and with the sun setting soon, it would be the first time in a month that Sarah could cast with us. It was our opportunity to do something.

My driveway was even more packed with cars than when I'd left. I drove up onto the grass and parked behind Betty's truck. I threw myself out of my car and barreled up the steps to my front door. Flinging it open, I ground to a halt as everyone's heads turned toward me.

The living room was packed with people. My eyes bounced from face to face. I wasn't sure how they all fit. Chairs had been pulled in from all over the house. Every seat was taken. I swallowed as my gaze traveled over them, taking inventory. My coven was there: Betty, Agnes, Sarah, Megan, and Heather. Sitting next to them were four other witches: Kim, Izzy, Grace, and my mother. Then there were the descendants: Jay, Noah, Kevin, and Bob. Charlie, my familiar, stalked around the room, his fluffy tail swishing. Finally, there was Chris, my rock, my everything.

My mouth was dry. I tried licking my lips to wet them. "How's everything going?"

Bob glowered at me and sipped from his flask. "Crowded."

"You got a sec?" Megan stood and cocked her head.

I followed her into the hallway.

Megan lowered her voice. "It's all set up in the woods behind your house. We were just waiting for the sun to set. Are you ready?"

"As ready as I'll ever be."

Megan squeezed my shoulder and stepped around me back into the living room. "A few of us ladies need to have a quick... book club meeting. Hang tight, and we'll do dinner after, okay?"

"Book club?" Kevin raised an eyebrow. "Is now the right time for that?"

"Yep." I looped my arm through Megan's and dragged her toward the back door. "We won't be long."

Every witch in the room stood and walked toward me. Lori grabbed Izzy's arm and shook her head.

"I want to—"

Lori shook her head. "It has to be just the descendants."

I stepped up next to my mom and dropped my voice to a whisper. Izzy was trying to do the right thing, and Lori was being a little rough about it. To smooth things over, I thought of the first excuse I could come up with. "If things go wrong, Chris will need backup in here. Please. Keep them safe."

Izzy studied my face. She narrowed her eyes and pressed her lips together then nodded and turned back to the room. She flopped down on the couch next to Heather.

Noah looked between her and me.

I smiled weakly. "She's behind in the reading."

"Okay..." Noah shrugged and sat back down. "Anyone want to play a card game?"

I turned from the room and followed the other witches out into the woods. We walked past the tree line and continued single file for about a hundred feet before a small clearing came into view. During the day, the other witches had cleared it further, chopping up the underbrush and leaving a clear spot in the center. White rocks had been gathered and built into a circle in the center of the space, with candles dispersed between the stones. At each of the four cardinal directions, something herbal and fragrant had been smeared across the rocks.

I walked around the circle, studying it. "How does this work?"

The rest of the coven spread out, spacing themselves

evenly around the circle as Lori moved to stand next to me. "We'll summon Meredith's spirit here, and the circle will help contain her—not like the prison back at her house, more like a waiting room." Lori pointed at the herb mixtures. "It's a charm designed to calm her. I know that sounds strange, but we need to be able to reach her. We need to help her let go so she can rest, so she can forgive. This helps separate her from the Outsider's influence so she can go back to who she was before this all began."

"A woman in pain?" I asked.

"A woman in love." Lori extended her hand to me.

I stared at it. All the other witches around me began reaching out, clasping hands with the person next to them. Grace slipped her hand into Lori's grasp. I sighed and took the offered hand. With my other hand, I reached out and grabbed Megan.

"Are you ladies ready?" Lori asked.

We all murmured confirmation. She nodded and took a step forward. We shuffled inward with her until the tips of our toes touched the circle of white stones. She began to hum next to me. We all joined in until our voices harmonized. Grace exhaled, releasing her purple sparkles into the air. They danced around the circle before stopping in front of Lori.

One by one, we each added our magic to the mix. To Grace's left was Kim. She added in her floating red spheres. Sarah added in flickering flames. Betty released her misshaped pearls. An iridescent haze floated out of Agnes's mouth. Megan released her flower petals. All the colors and lights swirled together into a vortex in front of Lori. Megan squeezed my hand, and I added my own golden motes of light. They flew out of me, almost as if they were being pulled. Last to join the mix were Lori's silver sparkles. The lights pulsed and grew until I had to close my eyes against the brightness.

Lori chanted the spell. We all joined in on the second verse, adding our voices to the call. "We call to thee. Appear before us, Meredith Walker!"

The lights pulsed brighter. Heat hit my face, then it dissipated.

"Traitors!" Meredith screeched.

I flinched and opened my eyes. Meredith stood in the center of the stones. The last time I'd seen her, she had been translucent and glowing a faint green color. Now, she almost looked solid. Her hair was fire-engine red with a white streak down one side. Her bright-green eyes were wide.

She spun slowly in the circle, her finger pointing at us as she continued to wail. "Traitors!"

Lori's fingers flexed around mine, her hands shaking as she murmured the words to the next spell. Her silver lights flowed into the circle. One by one, we followed suit, each of us adding the spell's power.

I clenched my fists, gripping Megan's and my mother's hands as I pushed my will into the spell. *Rest. Please just rest.*

Meredith.

I flinched as the word filtered through my mind. It was a thought, but it didn't belong to me. It was a whispered word by someone else inside my skull.

Meredith. The voice was beseeching and playful, like an invitation. I pushed it aside and tried to overwhelm whatever was happening with my own intention.

Someone screamed behind me.

I flinched and continued to hold onto Megan's hand. *Please work. Rest. Please rest.* I couldn't tell if it was just in my head, a noise designed to distract me.

Meredith. The voice that wasn't mine continued to echo in my skull, mingling with the sound of fear.

What's happening?

Another scream cut through the air.

Is that real?

Meredith turned toward me, a vicious smile on her lips. Then she disappeared.

"What...?" I stumbled forward, staring at the blank space where she had been. I spun toward my mother. "It didn't work."

Another scream.

My head jerked toward the sound, and my heart plummeted as I realized where it was coming from. The scream was very real, and it was coming from my house.

I ran. My legs carried me through the trees toward my home. The other women scurried behind me. Kim cursed under her breath as she tottered forward on her forearm crutches, trying her best to keep up. I quickly lost track of her as I pushed forward, throwing myself through the tree line and into my backyard.

It was like I had stumbled into a horror movie. My home was surrounded by shuffling shapes that I couldn't focus on long enough to tell if they were living or dead. The back door had been caved inward. Izzy stood in the threshold, her hands thrust out in front of her as she yelled wordlessly. Blue waves of magic poured from her, pushing the shapes away from the stairs. I paused for only a second to take it all in before I was dashing forward. Izzy's arms shook, her knees sagging weakly. I opened my mouth and yelled too. I willed my motes of light to surge toward Izzy and bolster her before she fell. They danced ahead of me as I ran across the grass.

As my magic hit Izzy, her eyes widened. A second later, red petals joined the mix. Izzy's hands shook, and she stumbled back from her position. She fell in the doorway, shaking her head, trying to clear it. On quivering arms, she pushed herself to her feet, but it was too late. The blue wave had failed, and the people in the yard rushed forward. I stumbled up the stairs. For half a second, I made eye contact with Bob before I spun and threw myself in front of Izzy. Sarah was hot on my heels. She skidded to a stop beside me, and before I could open my mouth to say a word, she lifted her hand and threw a fireball into the yard.

CHAPTER 14

I stood slack-jawed as Sarah inched ahead of me on the porch. It was like she was dancing. Her body shifted in smooth, fluid movements. With one hand, she whipped up the wind and hurled it toward the dark forms crowding the yard. With her other hand, she launched fireballs. Her magic, which was normally small flickers of flame, became a raging inferno around her. I had never seen so much magic coming off someone without another witch funneling their magic to boost them. Her raw talent mesmerized me.

Megan and Lori scrambled onto the porch next to her. They linked hands and began chanting. Lori's silver sparkles twirled between Megan's flower petals as they swept out along the tree line, containing the wind and the fire. Betty and Agnes followed suit, building up a barrier in front of the house to protect it from the heat rolling off Sarah's fires in the yard.

I stood still, my mind racing. Everything was happening so quickly.

Even Kim was in the fight. She leaned heavily on her forearm crutches as she threw ward after ward over my house. They kept breaking before they could fully settle into the wood. She continued on, though, casting another one before the last one had fully dissolved. Slowly, she gained traction.

Behind me, someone kept screaming. I jerked toward the sound and stumbled into the house as Izzy scrambled from the door to reenter the fray.

Inside the house was almost as chaotic as outside. Jay was sprawled across the living room floor. He was the one screaming, his eyes wide with panic. Noah knelt next to him, trying desperately to calm his friend. Kevin rocked back and forth in the corner, babbling. And Bob just stood there, his eyes wide, his flask on the ground at his feet.

Chris charged into the room from the hallway, a medical kit clasped to his chest. He slid to a stop next to Noah and flipped open the lid. "What do you need?"

I scrambled forward and crouched next to Jay. I stared into Noah's eyes as he reached for the kit.

"How bad is it?" I asked.

He shook his head. "A scratch."

I glanced down at Jay and found Noah was right. It was a scratch across his forearm. I had seen grazed knees worse than this. "What—"

Noah snorted and cleaned up the minor wound. "He's always had this irrational fear of zombies. When most people heard a random noise outside, we thought, 'I wonder if that was a raccoon.' He always wondered if it was a zombie."

Jay began to hyperventilate.

Noah pressed his forehead to his friend's. "Breathe, buddy. The zombies didn't scratch you. It was a piece of wood. You're fine."

"It's not irrational. It's not irrational." Jay pointed at the open doorway.

Noah continued to demonstrate calm breathing. "Remember the lore, right? Doesn't a zombie have to bite you?"

"Yes," Jay stammered.

"It was a scratch from a piece of flying wood. You'll be okay. We'll get through this. And look at the bright side. You've always enjoyed telling me 'I told you so.'"

Jay's breathing steadied, and he nodded.

I glanced behind me. Flashes of light still streamed in through the open doorway. The wind howled outside, but the barriers Betty and Agnes had put up kept it away from the windows. The fight continued, but it was contained.

I wiped my hands on my pants and stood. *This is all too much. Where's Delaney? Shouldn't she be here by now?* I had never thought I would want a Warden here, but we needed one. I yanked my phone from my pocket and dialed Miranda's number. It went straight to voicemail. "Miranda. We're under attack. Meredith is laying siege to my house. We need you." I hung up and strode toward the door.

As I stepped out onto the back porch, the yard was still. Sarah slumped, falling to her knees. Izzy slid to the floor next to her. The rest of the witches slowly made their way over to us, collapsing to their knees one by one as the exhaustion from casting so many spells back to back hit them.

I scanned the yard. It was too dark to see well. Clouds covered the full moon overhead. In the dim light, I could make out shapes in the yard, but none moved. I closed my eyes and focused on my body. My heart was still racing. But it was from adrenaline and didn't seem to be a sign that more was coming. Not right now anyway.

I stepped back into the house and walked as calmly as I could into the kitchen, where I collected my stash of protein bars and Snickers from the fridge. I strode back through the living room, past the wide-eyed Kevin and Jay, slipping around Chris, who was whispering comforting words to Bob, and back outside to my coven. I handed out the snacks so they could refuel. I grabbed the last protein bar and inhaled it while I stared out at the yard.

"We can't stay here," Kim said around a mouthful of Snickers. "If they come back, the wards on your house aren't strong enough to keep them out. And I don't have time to put the ones in place that you would need to keep everyone safe."

I held her gaze. "Where to, then?"

"My place." Kim's eyes were steady and sure.

"Good idea." I studied the cars in my driveway and began mentally doing the math. We didn't need to take them all. I stepped into the doorway and began pointing at people. "All right, we need to go someplace safer than here. Kim has very graciously offered up her home. Let's quickly pack and head out. Chris, could you drive Bob, Jay, and Noah? I'll take Grace, Megan, and Kevin." I pointed at Betty. "You can take Agnes and Sarah. Kim? Would you mind driving Izzy and Lori?"

"Yea—"

"Hold up." Noah put his hands on his hips. "I'm not going anywhere until you tell me what's going on."

I shook my head. "We don't have time—"

"Make time." Noah crossed his arms over his chest and glared at me.

I groaned. Meredith could come back at any minute. *Does she have the same refueling requirements as we do? Will she hit us again tonight?* I gritted my teeth. I could see why Kevin had had such a hard time convincing Noah to come here in the first place. He was stubborn. I dropped my arms to my sides and sighed. "I promise to answer all your questions. When we are someplace safe."

"When—"

Grace stepped in front of him, blocking his view of me. "Yes, when we are someplace safe. You have my word on it too."

He stared down at her, his expression softening. He

extended his hand toward her, his little finger raised. "Pinky promise?"

Grace chuckled and linked her finger with his. "Pinky promise."

"You know my first question is going to be why you always wear gloves, right?" Noah asked.

Grace ducked her head. "Don't worry. I'm not like Rogue from the X-Men. They're more to protect me than other people."

"Then I'll save that question for another day." He dropped her hand and turned to help Jay up from the floor.

"Are we good?" I looked around the room. Everyone was still tense, but they all met my eye and nodded. "Then let's get going."

We took ten minutes to pack our bags then filed out of my house. I did my best to close my back door before we left, though it had been broken off its hinges. I propped it closed and shuffled around the house toward my car, Grace, Charlie, and Megan in tow. Instead of Kevin sliding into my car, Noah claimed the last spot in the back seat next to my daughter. I glanced at him in the rear-view mirror. He stared out the passenger-side window the entire drive to Kim's home.

Kim led the caravan. She pulled as far forward in her long driveway as she could. The other vehicles piled in around her. We barely fit, but with only four vehicles, we made it work. I got out of my car and trudged up the walkway to her front door. The neighborhood was quiet. The clouds had moved, and the moon blanketed the yard in a warm glow. It was a beautiful night. It was almost hard to believe only a few minutes before, we had been facing down a vengeful ghost with undead at her disposal.

We piled into Kim's living room. A large sectional couch took up most of the room. While it was big, it wouldn't accommodate everyone. Megan darted into the other rooms, collecting chairs for people to sit on. Everyone but Noah collapsed into their seats, exhaustion clear in their eyes.

He just stood there, his arms crossed over his chest and his chin raised in a challenge. "Are we safe now?"

"For now." I slouched onto a hard wooden stool from the breakfast nook.

"So, what was that?"

I grimaced. While no law of magic forbade telling nonwitches about us, it was generally frowned upon. It was like the unspoken fifth law, behind don't attract the attention of Wardens. I had broken it for Heather and Chris, but this felt different. I didn't know the other descendants well. "Would you believe me if I said it was a gas leak?"

Noah snorted as Jay, Bob, and Kevin all murmured no's.

"I didn't think so." I sighed. *They deserve to know. Meredith's coming for them.* "We're witches."

Noah's expression shifted rapidly between surprise, incredulity, horror, and acceptance. He nodded, urging me to continue.

"Most of us are descended from the same coven. Other than Izzy. That original coven was made up of Hazel Hill"—I pointed toward Sarah—"Lillian Jones"—my finger tracked across the room to Kimberly—"Beatrice Taylor." I pointed to Betty next, followed by Megan, then Agnes. "Ruby Miller, Clara Price." I pointed to myself then Lori and Grace. "Edie Williams. And lastly… Meredith Walker."

Bob's head jerked up at her name, his eyes widening.

"Yeah. That Meredith," I said.

Noah looked between us. "Does someone want to fill me in on what *that Meredith* means?"

"She was in a relationship with a man named Booker Lancaster. He… he was murdered by your ancestors." I gestured toward Jay, Kevin, Bob, and finally Noah. "She really wanted revenge, so she made a deal with something that is hard to explain. It gave her a bunch of power, and her original coven tried to stop her. They locked her up in a magical prison. She escaped. And now she wants to kill us all."

Noah nodded. "Okay. Let me get this straight. You're all witches, except for apparently you." He pointed at Heather, who nodded. "And another witch is coming for us?"

"Technically, a ghost of a witch," Lori said.

"Right. A ghost of a witch. Because that makes sense." Noah nodded again. "Magic is real?"

Grace hugged her arms to her body. "Yes. Is that a problem?"

He shook his head. "No. I mean, this is an awful situation. But I've got to be honest, that's the coolest thing I've ever heard. Magic's real. That's... awesome."

"Really?" Grace peered at him through her eyelashes.

"Yeah." He inched toward her, a smile spreading across his lips. "It makes you even cooler than you already were."

Grace flushed and looked away.

I cleared my throat to get his attention again. "Meredith won't stop unless we stop her. We're working to contain and banish her. We just need to keep you all safe until we can get the job done."

"Anything we can do to help?" Kevin asked.

"I'm going to assume follow directions." Noah flopped down on the couch next to Jay. "And now that I know why, I'm totally cool with that."

"Any other questions?" I asked.

Bob cleared his throat. "Have any of your investigations involved people using magic?"

I met his gaze. "Yes."

He nodded and looked down at the floor.

The room fell into a contemplative silence as everyone mulled over the evening's events. Kevin sat stock-still in the corner, his eyes wide. Bob found his flask and drank from it, his brow furrowed. Charlie wound his way through the room, rubbing against everyone's legs in an attempt to calm them.

Chris stepped up next to me and wrapped his arms around my waist. "Not to repeat the question, but what can we do to help?"

I leaned into him. "I think we all need to rest. We've got a small window of opportunity to banish her. It has to be done on a full moon. But we are all running on fumes, and if we want to stand a chance, we have to recharge. Let's make up some beds, crash, and we can start this fresh in the morning."

Chris kissed the top of my head. "Deal."

We took another minute to collect ourselves before we all stood and began arranging the room for people to sleep. Kim had a spare room but not enough space for everyone. Grace and Izzy claimed floor space in Kim's daughter's room, and Noah and Jay were invited to stay in the son's room. Her two kids helped make up the beds before groggily shuffling back to bed. The Retirees were given the guest room. Megan and Lori made up pallets in Kim's office, while Bob, Heather, Chris, Kevin, and I split up the living room. After making up a spot for me and Chris on the floor, I slipped out of the room and padded down the hall to the dining room, where the other witches had gathered. I'd heard their murmurs from my spot on the floor. I was the last to enter.

Heather was there. She had made tea for everyone. She slid a mug into my hands after I claimed a spot on the floor. I looked around the room. Everyone was staring at me again, waiting for me to speak. I sipped the chamomile. It warmed me from the inside, releasing some of the tension in my shoulders. Charlie flopped down next to me and curled into my side. I rested my hand on his side, scratching him mindlessly under his chin as I pondered the night's events.

"What went wrong?" I asked.

Lori sagged into her chair. "I don't know. It was almost

exactly like I saw it in my dreams. The circle. The words. But in my dreams, it worked."

I sipped my drink again. "Almost?"

Lori shrugged. "It's always dark out, but now that I think about it, I don't remember trees."

"So we were in the wrong place?" Megan asked.

Lori shrugged again. "All the research I've done doesn't indicate the location is important. It's the people, the spell preparations. It should have worked."

I closed my eyes and replayed the events. Everything had broken down with that voice in my head. *Meredith.* Like someone had placed the thought inside my brain. It wasn't my voice. "Did anyone else hear someone calling her? Not out loud, though. In your head."

I looked around the room as everyone nodded.

Kim straightened in her seat. "It was like someone was calling her away."

Betty inched forward. "The Outsider is still out there. It must have messed with the ritual somehow. Maybe it was summoning her out of it, like we were summoning her into it?"

Sarah tapped her chin. "It makes sense. We have to deal with it before we can recapture Meredith."

All eyes moved back to me. I was the one assigned to investigation duties. It was on me to get it right. I fidgeted. Charlie pushed himself against my hip and purred, vibrating against me. Setting my drink down, I scooped him up to hold him. I pressed my face into his fur. I wasn't sure where to go with the investigation from here. *Should I look for more missing people? Should I investigate the deaths that have already happened?* I felt like I was floundering.

"I'll continue investigating tomorrow. I'm too exhausted to think tonight," I said. "Either way, we need to get ready to cast the spell again. I'll team up with Chris. I think the rest of you should focus on getting ready so we can try again."

The other women murmured their agreement, and we broke up for the night. I slipped into my pallet on the floor next to Chris. He wrapped his arms around me. I lay there in the darkness, listening to him sleep behind me. I nestled into the pile of warm blankets, breathing in the scent of lemon balm. In the morning, I would have to continue pressing forward. But for right now, I felt safe in his arms, snuggled in a pile of blankets, with Charlie wrapped around my head.

CHAPTER 15

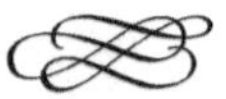

I woke to the scent of bacon. My stomach rumbled, and I crawled out from under Chris's arm and stumbled toward the kitchen. I shuffled into the room, yawning, and collapsed onto a chair at the counter. Heather was flipping pancakes at the stove. She had three pans going at once and was creating a mountain of food on the counter.

"So, I've been wondering for days and haven't found a good time to ask, how did he do it?" Heather slid another pancake onto the stack and poured more batter.

I yawned. "Do what?"

"Ask you to marry him."

"Oh." I flushed. "He didn't."

Heather gasped and spun toward me, her eyes wide and her mouth open in shock. "Dani! You didn't! You asked him?"

I nodded.

She squealed and darted across the room to pull me into a hug. "Congratulations! Oh my gosh. Tell me what happened. How did you get from breaking the l-word seal to being engaged?"

Up until that evening, I hadn't told Chris I loved him. I'd only had the courage to go through with it because Heather had encouraged me to. I wasn't sure how it had escalated from that to a marriage proposal so quickly. But I didn't regret it. I opened and closed my mouth a few times before I could get the words out. "I told him I wanted to spend the rest of my life with him."

"And?"

"He… he joked that it sounded like a marriage proposal. But once the word 'proposal' was out there, it became one." I covered my face with my hands. "I don't know. I didn't plan it. It wasn't the most romantic proposal, but he said yes. And I couldn't be happier."

Heather scurried back to the stove to check on the pancakes. "He would have been crazy to say no. You two are perfect together."

I beamed at her. With everything going on, it was nice to have that moment of normalcy. "Do you want to be my maid of honor?"

"Yes!" Heather spun back toward me. "I'll plan the best bachelorette party ever."

While neither of us was particularly wild when it came to parties, Heather's skill at baking might only be surpassed by that of Abby or Willow, who were both professional chefs. And it was a toss-up on the best of days. I was pretty much guaranteed to have the tastiest party, which would honestly make it the best. "I wouldn't doubt it."

Heather rattled off snack ideas for the various events surrounding weddings as she continued making breakfast. We hadn't even set a date, and she was already planning a cookie bar for the engagement party. I couldn't keep the smile off my face as she pulled the bacon out of the oven.

"All right. Breakfast is done." Heather pulled off the apron she had been wearing. "I should probably head out. Becca agreed to open, but I don't want to strand her there alone during the rush."

"Thanks for giving me a normal morning," I said.

She smiled at me on her way out. "Anytime."

As the front door closed behind her, I pulled out my phone to check my work schedule. As an independent claims adjuster, I got to set my own hours. Fortunately, while investigating the last case, I had pushed out all my inspections. I didn't have anything on my calendar for a couple more days. I quickly responded to a few work emails before dropping my phone next to my plate and digging in to the breakfast Heather had made.

Chris slumped into the seat next to me. He had bags under his eyes as he rubbed his face and reached for a piece of my bacon. He munched on it as he ran his fingers through his hair to tame it. "I've got to head in to work in a few minutes."

I chewed my eggs. It was funny how the world worked. Our lives were blowing up around us, and we still had to go in to work. The world could be ending, and we would still have to go in to work. The need to be productive didn't stop for anyone.

"Did you want to tag along to my first stop of the morning?" Chris asked.

"Where are you going?" I asked.

"Victor's." Victor was the local medical examiner. Chris stood and poured two mugs of coffee. "He messaged me this morning and said he found something interesting."

I surged to my feet. "Yeah, let's go."

Chris chuckled and handed me one mug. "It can wait until after we're done eating."

The medical examiner's office hadn't changed in years. It was housed at the back of a funeral home. The house itself looked no different from the others on the block—except for the unusual chimney at the back, where Victor had a crematorium. The rest of it was quaint, a two-story craftsman with beige walls and calming decorations. Everything about the waiting room was bland, from the wall color to the dull banister wood. In stark contrast, Victor himself looked quite eccentric in Regency-era clothing, with his white hair styled into an impressive pompadour. His beard was always neatly trimmed, and his blue eyes twinkled. He was almost like a gothic Santa—a handsome, athletic, gothic Santa.

Victor wasn't behind the desk when we arrived. Instead, it was his newest assistant. She wore a polka-dot dress with a high collar. Her purple hair was piled into a loose bun on top of her head. She looked as eccentric as her new mentor. Chris stopped in front of the desk and got her attention.

She smiled at him. It was a practiced, sympathetic smile. People were rarely happy at a funeral home, and it seemed like she was already used to being a calming presence. "Can I help you, sir?" she asked.

Chris flashed his badge. "Victor should be expecting me."

The assistant nodded and gestured to the waiting room. "He's back there with Mr. Ellison's family. He'll be right with you."

I followed Chris to the waiting room, and we sat, perched on the edge of the fainting couch together until Victor emerged from the back. Two women trailed him. The first woman was about my height, maybe a little taller at five foot six. Her brown hair was pulled into a low ponytail that hung loose over her shoulder. Her hazel eyes were red rimmed, and she wiped at them with a crumpled tissue.

Next to her, holding her hand, was a second woman. The second woman was short, barely five feet. Her jet-black hair was cut into an asymmetrical bob, with the undersides shaved. The tips of her hair were dyed a deep plum that matched her bold makeup. While the first woman was dressed in sensible pumps with a pencil skirt and a cream blouse, the other wore combat boots, with an oversized sweatshirt that covered most of her body. On the center of her chest was graffiti-style art and a chunky necklace that looked almost like a pixelized sun.

Chris stood. I scrambled to my feet next to him and hovered at the side of the group as he shook the women's hands. "I'm the deputy investigating your father's case. Would you mind waiting a few minutes? I have a couple of things to discuss with Mr. Shaw, but I have a few questions for you both if you have time."

The two women exchanged a look and nodded. They shuffled past Chris and claimed the couch behind me. Chris followed Victor from the room.

I hovered for a second before claiming the stiff-backed chair opposite the couch. I made eye contact with the woman with hazel eyes. "I'm sorry to hear about your father."

She wiped at her face. "My father? Ray wasn't my father."

The woman with the asymmetrical bob smiled weakly. "He was mine."

My eyes widened, and I opened my mouth like a fish out of water. Talk about foot in mouth. But they looked nothing alike.

The more colorful one of the two lowered her gaze. "I know. No family resemblance, right? I was adopted. Just like my dad. I'm Ji'an, by the way. And this is Alison. She and my dad worked together."

The hair on the back of my neck stood up at the word *adopted.* I shivered and inched forward in my seat, trying to find a comfortable position. "Nice to meet you both. I didn't know Ray was adopted. Did he ever meet his birth parents? Sorry if that's a rude question. It's just not every day you meet someone so open about being adopted."

Ji'an peered up at me through her lashes as she chewed on her nails. "He went to some agency in town. I don't remember the name. They wouldn't tell him anything, though. Said it was a closed adoption and they couldn't reveal names."

I softened my voice. "That must have been hard on him."

Ji'an shrugged and pulled the sleeves of her sweatshirt down to cover her hands. "It was more a curiosity for him. He didn't mind not knowing. He always said he had the best family a guy could ask for—loving parents, a happy home. He adopted me because he wanted to pass the love down the line. His favorite thing to say was that every kid deserves to feel wanted. And adopted kids? They're lucky because they're always wanted."

I smiled at her. It was a beautiful sentiment. The adoption process was long and required a lot of paperwork. No one went into it lightly. It was a sweet way to look at it versus how so many others did. Instead of focusing on the giving-up portion, Ray had focused on the receiving end. We chatted for a few more minutes about her dad. He was a dentist. He was a little disappointed she hadn't followed in his footsteps, but digital art was more fun. She animated video games for a living. Alison was a friend from high school, and she had stumbled into being a receptionist for his dental office.

After about ten minutes, Chris emerged from the back room. He took the seat next to me and crossed his hands over his knee. "Are you both still up for answering a few questions?"

Ji'an and Alison pulled together, clasping each other's hands as they nodded.

I slipped backward in my seat and tried to give them the illusion of privacy as I became small in my chair.

Chris pulled out his notebook and flipped it open. "Can either of you think of someone who would have wanted to hurt Ray?"

Ji'an shook her head. "Everyone loved him."

Alison pursed her lips. "Not really. He never mentioned

having issues with anyone. He was everyone's favorite dentist. And that's something. Not everyone enjoys the dentist. He had a way of making it less scary."

Chris nodded and looked at Alison. "I understand you were the last person to see Ray alive. Did he seem—"

"I wasn't the last."

Chris paused, his pen hovering over the page. "You weren't?"

"No." She crossed her ankles. "The last I saw him, it was the end of the workday. He was at the end of the parking lot, talking to an older woman. They were still talking when I left."

"An older woman?" Chris asked.

The pressure in my skull pulsed. I stiffened in my seat and listened carefully to her response.

Alison nodded again. "Yeah. White hair, an old-fashioned blue dress. It was a bit long for the weather, but to each their own."

"Do you know who she was?"

Alison pursed her lips. "I didn't recognize her. She didn't look well. He was pointing down the street. I kind of assumed he was giving her directions to the urgent care. It's in the same direction. So, I guess I'm the last person who knew him who saw him alive. But I wasn't technically the last. That woman was."

Chris asked a few more follow-up questions. Their answers passed in a blur. Eventually, the questions came to an end, and I followed Chris out to our cars. I linked my hand with Chris's as we walked down the funeral home's front steps.

My mind was focused on Alison's description of the woman. She didn't look like she felt well. I chewed on my lip. Justin hadn't looked well either when the Outsider had been possessing him. *What if this woman is the latest host?*

"Did you pick up on anything in there?" Chris asked.

"Two things," I said as we came to stop next to Chris's car. "First, Ray's adopted. That felt important for some reason. And two, the old woman. I got a strange feeling when she was being described. I can't help but think she's a Justin 2.0. How about you? What did Victor find?"

Chris settled back against his car door. "He confirmed that both Raymond Ellison and Jennifer Moore were killed with the same murder weapon. It was a three-sided dagger. He thinks it may have ceremonial importance."

I nodded. A ceremonial dagger made sense with a ritual circle.

"And—"

"There's more?"

"Yeah. And he is fairly certain they were both killed by the same person. He used a bunch of medical jargon, but it involved stab patterns and wound depth. He's working on figuring out the killer's height. He's ruled out anyone over six feet and hopes to have a more precise estimate soon."

I rested my head against his shoulder and closed my eyes.

"Back to work?" he asked.

"Yeah."

"Me too." Chris wrapped his arm around me. "I'll look into the adoption angle. I might be able to find the name of the agency."

I gave him a quick kiss then pulled away and strode back to my car. "And I'll see if I can figure out who the older woman is. I'll update you as soon as I find something."

Under six feet didn't necessarily mean a woman, but I had a feeling the Outsider was wearing one, except my list of potentials didn't have any older women. I needed to take a second look at the list of missing persons and obituaries. I was willing to bet her name would be somewhere on that list.

CHAPTER 16

When I pulled into Kim's driveway, Heather's car was there. I let myself in and followed my nose to the kitchen. The buttery scent of croissants made my mouth water. Heather was unpacking trays of baked goods onto the counter—chocolate-filled croissants, breakfast sandwiches, and a mound of cookies. She dropped a large jug of coffee next to it all and took a step back. Everyone hovered around the edges of the kitchen. The second she stepped back, they descended like locusts, grabbing up the delicious baked goods before scurrying to find a place to sit before all the good chairs were taken.

I grinned at the sight. Despite the stressful night, a delicious breakfast made everyone forget for a few minutes. I snagged a breakfast sandwich before everything was gone and settled against the back wall to eat it.

"I thought I had made enough." Heather claimed a spot next to me. "But Noah called and said it was almost gone. I forgot to account for how big young men's and kids' appetites can be. Apparently, Kim's son ate six pancakes by himself before he left for school."

I chuckled as I continued to eat.

"How'd things go at the funeral home?" Heather bumped me with her shoulder. "Chris was grumbling about how early Victor had called as I was heading out."

"Funeral home?" Noah asked.

I eyed him over my food. Normally, I would have pulled my coven aside to discuss next steps. I got the distinct impression he would object to that. He was annoyingly strong willed, it seemed. I bit into my sandwich, taking my time to respond. He held my gaze as I chewed. Definitely strong willed.

"We got two leads. Chris is tracking down the first, and I'll focus on the second."

Bob snorted.

I smiled weakly and took another bite of my sandwich.

"Which is?" Noah asked.

I sighed. "You remember last night when I mentioned Meredith made a deal with something?"

All the men turned to stare at me. Noah nodded.

"Well, that something is capable of possessing dead bodies. The last time we dealt with it, we—"

Bob gaped at me. "Did you just say possessing dead bodies?"

I pushed away from the wall and poured myself a cup of coffee. "Yeah. Remember Julie? Well, her weapon of choice was the Outsider possessing her brother's body. And the last time we dealt with it, the possession left this strange magical residue everywhere. We think the same thing's happening. But maybe sans residue this time. We think the Outsider has gotten better at what it does. And my lead gave me an idea of what its current host might look like—an older woman, white hair."

I returned to my spot against the back wall. Bob had slumped into his seat and was staring at his cup, his eyes unblinking. Kevin fidgeted in his seat, and Jay looked as white as a sheet. Noah nodded along with a contemplative look.

"How are you so cool about all of this?" I asked.

Noah blinked. "Oh, I'm not. I'm internally freaking out, but my job as a grief counselor requires me to deal with stressful situations all the time. I'm saving my meltdown for later."

"Useful skill."

"Looks like you're doing the same. So, what's next? How do we find this older woman?" Noah asked.

I pulled out my phone. "Search missing person reports, obituaries, crime blogs, that sort of thing. We're looking for someone who might be dead that fits the bill."

He grabbed his phone. "Old woman who died. Got it. What time frame are we looking for?"

"Sometime over the last month," I responded.

The room fell into silence as we scrolled through the various news sites. When we stumbled across a possible match, we called out the name. Each name seemed to lead to a dead end as we pulled up photos and the hair wasn't right or the timeline didn't make sense. After twenty minutes of searching, Noah announced he thought he had found her.

"Susan Thompson, age eighty-two. Died three weeks ago."

He flipped his phone around so we could see the picture. It wasn't a news article but a photo someone had sent him through text.

"Where'd you get that?" Grace asked.

He grabbed the back of his neck. "My job requires being involved in grief support groups. Her son's a member of one. Normally, I wouldn't share anything that comes up in those groups. It's unethical. But I figured these were extenuating circumstances. If something's possessing his mom, I'm sure Mark would be horrified."

I looked her up online. She had a limited social media

presence. Most of her posts were of her grandkids or great-grandkids. She liked to knit sweaters for dogs. Her family had posted several sad messages about how she would be missed but nothing about where she was buried. I scrolled through the photos and paused when a familiar face popped up. I squinted down at the phone. Olivia, the insurance agent who worked across the hall from me, had her arm around Susan's shoulders. Her smile was big and bright. Her black hair was twisted into a thick braid. I continued to scroll and found a second photo from a few months prior. Olivia was in it again. They were at some sort of charity function together.

I texted Olivia.

DANI:
Sorry if this is a rude question, but do you know where Susan Thompson is buried? I wanted to pay my respects.

OLIVIA:
She isn't. Her memorial service is today. I didn't realize you knew each other.

DANI:
Not well. I just heard.

OLIVIA:
Did you want to come? I'm sure the family would love to see more people there.

DANI:
If you don't think they will mind.

OLIVIA:
Not at all. I'll send you the information.

I put my phone back down and grabbed my coffee. It was lukewarm as I sipped it. My hands shook. Sticking my nose where it wasn't wanted was always uncomfortable. Part of me hoped for Mark's sake that I didn't find anything unusual at the memorial service. Selfishly, most of me hoped I would.

"You okay?" Heather asked.

I nodded. "I just got an invite to her memorial service. It's this afternoon."

I looked down at my clothes and blanched. When we'd fled from my house the night before, I hadn't thought about packing clothes for a funeral. All of my outfits were practical—jeans and T-shirts. The thought of going back to my house for a change of clothes made my stomach roil.

"I might have something that could work." Kim retreated from the room, her crutches clicking against the ground as she disappeared down the hallway.

I finished eating my breakfast sandwich and downed the rest of my coffee. I willed myself to stand still while I waited for Kim to return with a change of clothes. I was a natural fidgeter, but I didn't want to raise the tension in the room. Everyone was sitting around the dining room table and in the adjoining kitchen, their shoulders hunched more than normal. Folding chairs had appeared while I was at the funeral home. Every spare inch of space had been taken up with seats. They huddled together, worry lines marring every face.

Megan sighed and leaned in her chair, rolling her shoulders back. "Do you have an ETA on when the Wardens are supposed to arrive? Shouldn't they be here by now?"

I shrugged. "Maybe they're waiting in the wings to clean it up once it blows up in our faces."

"Hasn't it already?" Agnes muttered.

"I tried calling again last night. It went straight to voicemail," I said.

Megan grunted, and her brow furrowed even more.

Lori folded in on herself, becoming as small as possible. When she spoke, her voice was barely above a whisper. "I hate to say it, but maybe we should call in Edith Voss."

"Who's Edith?" I asked.

Somehow, Lori became even smaller in her seat. She

tucked her legs up onto her chair and wrapped her arms around them. "Technically, she's retired. She was a Warden back in the day. She's... a bit prickly. But when I was doing my research, her name came up a few times. She was on the original team that put the bindings on Meredith."

"Why didn't you call her first?" Noah asked.

Lori rested her head on her knees and closed her eyes. "She was an enforcer. Her coming here isn't a good option. But I feel like we're out of those."

"We should put it to a vote." I pushed myself away from the wall and raised my hand. "All in favor of calling Edith Voss, raise your hand."

I glanced around the room. One by one, hands went up. The first was Noah's, followed by Izzy, then Grace, Heather, Betty, Agnes, and Sarah. Megan waffled for a few more seconds, her hand going up and down next to her head before she committed and raised it fully.

"The ayes have it." I lowered my hand. "Make the call."

Lori extracted her phone from her pocket and pressed it to her ear. She squeezed her eyes shut as it rang. It was like the whole room held its collective breath, our ears straining to hear. It was so silent, I could hear my mother's slow inhale and exhale and the ringtone on the other end. On the fourth ring, someone picked up. They didn't say anything.

With her eyes still closed, Lori exhaled sharply. "Meredith Walker has escaped."

The voice on the other end was muffled, but it had a harsh edge. "I'm on my way."

The line went dead, and Lori tossed her phone away from her onto the dining room table like it was a hot potato. She glowered at it and hugged her knees even harder to her chest, her fingers digging into her calves.

"That felt almost too easy," I said.

"I don't see good things happening from her coming."

Lori's eyes darted to Grace before she ducked her head to hide her face.

Kim shuffled back into the room with a black dress draped over her forearm. She stopped in the doorway, her eyes narrowing. "What did I miss?"

"A Hail Mary pass." I made my way over to her and collected the dress. "Thank you so much for letting me borrow this."

I scurried away down the hallway as Megan explained behind me. I wasn't sure if we had just made the right decision. Calling in two Wardens was bad enough. But we had just contacted a third. All bad things seemed to come in threes.

I shut the door to the bathroom behind me and quickly changed into the dress Kim had found for me. It was a modest black dress that hit just below the knees. It had a high-collared neckline with a cute bow. The flattering cut cinched at the waist. I studied myself in the mirror. This would do nicely for a funeral.

My phone dinged in my jeans pocket on the floor. I crouched to retrieve it. On the screen was a text message from Chris.

> **CHRIS:**
> Point Pleasant Family Planning and Adoption.
>
> I couldn't find the name of his parents. The records are sealed, and it'll take a few days to unseal them

As I stood, I discovered the dress had pockets. I slipped my phone and keys into one and patted them to make sure they weren't too obvious. The dress lay flat over them. I raised my eyebrow at my reflection. *Nice dress, Kim.*

I gathered my clothes and slipped out of the bathroom. I padded down the hall. The large group was still gathered in the dining room and kitchen. I studied the group from the hallway. Kim's poor house was packed to the gills. Seated at the dining room table proper were Grace, Lori, Noah, Jay, and Megan. Perched awkwardly on folding chairs along the walls were Bob, Kevin, and Izzy. And standing, balanced on her crutches in the middle of the kitchen, was Kim. They all looked exhausted.

I stepped into the doorway, and all eyes found me. Somehow, I had been placed in charge once more. I slipped past the group into the living room and dropped off my clothes, tucking them away into my overnight bag before returning and taking my spot along the far wall. Everyone in the room tracked my movements.

I straightened and began giving directions. "All right. Lori, Megan, can you start preparing for the ritual again? Betty, Agnes, and Sarah, I think we need to make sure we have some personal protections in place just in case. And maybe something the men can wield if they need to protect themselves. Can you make some potions? Kim, please check on your wards to make sure they won't be tested too much. Grace, I hate to ask this of you, but I need you to hold down the fort. You're the best at reading people, and I need you to let me or Heather know if everyone's stress gets to be too much. I'll send in Charlie, or Heather can work her own style of magic—calming people down."

The group mumbled their agreement. Izzy raised her hand. "Where do you want me?"

Sarah smiled at her. "Come help us. We could always use another set of hands."

"And we'll just stay here, I guess?" Noah asked.

"It's temporary." I looked at the Retirees. "Unless more hands would be helpful?"

"We can always use more hands," Betty said.

Agnes nodded. "Give us ten minutes to figure out what we're going to make, then we'll put you all to work."

"Excellent." Noah smiled and backed out of the room to give them space to think. He flopped down on the coach.

A minute later, Jay joined him.

The group disbanded to handle their respective assignments. I looked back at the adoption agency name Chris gave me as well as the details Olivia had sent me about the memorial service. I had a few hours before it started, which would give me plenty of time to swing by the adoption agency and hopefully sweet-talk them into giving me a clue.

CHAPTER 17

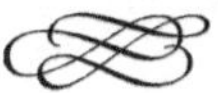

The adoption agency was two blocks from my office. I had probably passed it a hundred times and never noticed the place. It was on the second floor of a Brownstone building. Only a small sign inside the lobby, indicated what it was. I walked up the narrow flight of stairs and paused in the open doorway. Stacks of boxes filled the room. Plastic sheeting covered one wall, and the air was filled with recently disturbed dust. I inched my way past the boxes. They were piled everywhere, half covering the reception desk, which was otherwise empty. I rechecked the business listing online. I was in the right space, and it claimed the business was still open for another few hours.

I padded through the room, following the sound of someone breathing heavily in the back room. I rounded the corner and stopped when a woman came into view. She had short, graying, dirty-blond hair that had fallen forward, covering most of her face. She was bent over a filing cabinet, huffing as she manhandled a stack of files into a box at her feet. Her bright-red blazer lay forgotten at her bare feet, a pair of sensible kitten heels kicked off to the side. She froze and straightened when I entered the room.

Her hands flew over herself, tugging her shirt into place and tucking her hair behind her ears as she peered at me through thick-rimmed glasses. She strode forward, her hand thrust out in front of her. "Lisa Pratt. If you're here looking to adopt, I'm afraid to say you're a day too late. Well, more than a day. Technically, three months. We're closing our doors."

I shook her hand and stumbled over my words. "Oh, I'm—"

"I'm retiring, you see." Lisa released my hand and gestured toward the boxes. Her hands didn't stop moving the entire time she spoke. "I promised my husband we would travel and all that. Did you need a referral? I can make one for you. I know everyone worth knowing in the business, and several who aren't, so I can tell you which firms to stay away from."

"I—"

"Not that I have anything bad to say about them, mind you. So, a referral?" Lisa continued, her hands moving a mile a minute.

I coughed. "I'm actually investigating a recent crime."

Lisa ground to a halt. It was like the cogs were spinning in her head, and she had to pause for a moment for her thoughts to catch up. She straightened and stepped back. "A crime? What crime?"

"A murder," I said.

She covered her mouth, her eyes bugging out, then she paced back and forth in front of me. "A murder? That brings you here? What for? Were they looking to adopt? Oh gosh. I hope it wasn't one of my clients. I know all of them. Well, not well. But I know them. They're good families. Who was it?"

I held myself still to act as a counterbalance to her energy. "His name was Raymond Ellison. We're trying to rule out any connections to his biological family."

She inhaled sharply and froze again. This time, as the

cogs caught up, her eyes watered. A single tear trickled down her cheek. "I remember him. He was one of the first I did on my own, though my mother walked me through the process. She was a great attorney. His adoptive family sent me pictures. He seemed like a sweet kid."

I clasped my hands in front of me. "Can you tell me anything about the family that gave him up for adoption?"

She shook her head emphatically. "No. Client–attorney privilege. Unfortunately, I can't tell you anything about them without a warrant or subpoena. I wish I could be of more help."

"Are they still in the area?" I asked.

She pressed her lips together. "His adoption was a long time ago. I doubt there would be any connection to who put him up for adoption. If you ask me, you're barking up the wrong tree."

I studied her. A tingle started at the base of my spine and spread through my torso. Every nerve was on edge. I wet my lips. "How can you be so sure?"

"It was a long time ago," she said again.

A shiver went down my spine, and pressure pulsed at the base of my skull. I narrowed my eyes. *She knows something.* "What are all the boxes for?"

"Like I said. We're closing. The movers will be here in the morning. But don't worry. It's all going into storage. If you come back with a subpoena, everything will still be available. I can give you my email if you need. I'll be checking it periodically. To make referrals and whatnot."

"That would be lovely."

Lisa marched over to her blazer on the floor and pulled out a business card from a holder. She thrust it toward me. "Good luck with your investigation. Ray was a sweet kid. I hope you find out what happened to him."

I took the card and retreated to the stairs. Lisa was an interesting woman. I couldn't tell if she was stonewalling me or just eccentric. *Perhaps it's somewhere in the middle?* I stopped in front of my car and looked up at the building. It was a corner unit with a metal fire escape on the side. I chewed on my nails. *The records will be gone tomorrow. Should I...?* I clamped down on the thought before it took root. Breaking and entering was bad. It could cost Chris the position as sheriff if I was caught. *But I wouldn't be stealing anything. So is it always wrong?* I sighed and walked away before I could make a bad decision.

I left my car parked where it was and walked the two blocks to my office to meet up with Olivia. I crossed our shared lobby space and entered her office for Pleasant View Insurance Agency. Bailey, her golden retriever–pit bull mix, was sprawled on the floor, her stomach exposed to the room, fast asleep. Her legs twitched as she chased something in her dreams. Olivia stood from her desk. She wore a black dress with sensible pumps. Her dark hair was straightened and held back in a tight ponytail, her edges slicked back to prevent flyaways.

She locked up behind us, leaving Bailey napping, and we strolled the few blocks up to the Universalist church where Susan Thompson's funeral was being held. I stuck close to Olivia's side as we entered the building. It felt more like a celebration-of-life ceremony than a funeral. Groups of people congregated along the walls. Almost everyone held a cup of coffee or a small baked good as they talked. The voices were light. Despite the red-rimmed eyes, people wore small smiles as we passed. I listened in to a few of the groups as we made our way around the room. Everyone was talking about her and sharing some sort of story. It felt like she was everyone's grandma.

Olivia led me to the back of the room, where the mood

was more somber. We stopped in front of a balding gentleman. He wore a sweater-vest over slacks. Bifocals perched on the bridge of his nose. He had a youthful smile, though, when he looked up at us and saw Olivia, making it hard to place his age. He could have been anywhere from thirty to sixty, meaning he was either the son or a grandson.

"Dani, this is Mark," Olivia introduced me.

The son. I shook his hand. "My condolences for your loss."

"Thank you so much for coming," he said.

We exchanged a few more pleasantries before I disentangled myself from the conversation and slipped back into the crowd. I studied Mark from a distance. His grief felt real but somehow restrained. I relaxed my eyes and scanned the room for signs of magic. The space was well lit. I could sense the magic energy that surrounded all people but nothing out of the normal. Blinking away bright spots from accidentally looking at the light, I meandered around the edges of the memorial service, my fingers darting out to slide against recently touched objects. The whole room was filled with a deep melancholy, tinged with a bittersweet happiness. They were all here remembering the good times. It was a heady mix.

I slid my hands into my pockets and approached the back of the room, where an open doorway let to the inner sanctuary. Fewer people gathered in the next room. It was a steady line that moved slowly toward an open casket at the back. I faltered in the doorway. I didn't know Susan. It felt awkward enough being at her memorial service. But making the trek up to the casket made my heart clench. It was an invasion of privacy in a way. Everyone in attendance was there because she meant something to them. Saying goodbye was a private moment. I couldn't decide if me witnessing or participating in it was an affront or not.

"Excuse me," a woman behind me murmured.

I stepped to the side and let her enter the line, vacillating at the precipice for a few more seconds before I stepped up behind her. I had to know if any magical residue lingered on Susan's body. And so long as I was respectful, it would be okay. *Wouldn't it?* I kept my head down and crept through the room, following the line as it shuffled forward. People approached one by one or in pairs. The front of the line gave a good six feet of distance between it and the grieving visitor. Each person took a minute before they stepped to the side and followed the wall back the way we'd come. After a few minutes, I reached the front.

My brows creased as I stepped up next to the casket. In the photo Noah had found, she'd had stark-white hair. But the woman before me had dyed it a brilliant pink. She had been dressed in a fun dress that reminded me of Ms. Frizzle. It was bright and bold with dinosaurs all over it. Lying gently on her chest were crocheted flowers. This woman looked nothing like the description. I relaxed my eyes and checked for magical residue just to be sure. There was nothing. I stepped closer and lowered my voice. "You were loved. And you look like you were a lot of fun. I wish I could have known you."

With that, I retreated from the casket and followed the footsteps of those who had paid their respects before me. Once I had made it out to the main area, I ducked into the bathroom to text my coven.

DANI:
Susan isn't the new host.

BETTY:
What's next?

DANI:
I'm not sure. The adoption agency is closing, and I couldn't convince the owner to give me any information on the biological family.

> **MEGAN:**
> Maybe we should take a peek at the records after hours.

I stared wide-eyed at her suggestion. The thought had crossed my mind while I was at the agency, but it was a step further than I had gone before.

> **AGNES:**
> It's not like you would be removing anything. Just looking.

> **SARAH:**
> Izzy has volunteered to help.

Dani: How is the ritual prep going?

> **MEGAN:**
> Slowly. We probably won't be done until sometime tomorrow.

My hands hovered over the screen. I exhaled slowly through my mouth. They were right. It was just looking, and lives were on the line. If I was careful, no one would know, and it wouldn't impact Chris at all.

DANI:
Have Izzy meet me at my office at sunset.

I stared at my phone. Sarah gave my message a thumbs-up. My heart skipped a beat, and I shoved my phone back into my pocket. *It's just looking around. I've snooped before.* That thought didn't comfort me as I stepped out of the bathroom and rejoined the memorial service. While I had snooped before, I had always technically been invited in first. With each passing minute, I became more and more aware of what I would be doing that evening: breaking into the adoption agency office.

CHAPTER 18

With no other threads to pull on for my investigation, I headed back to my office. I spent the remainder of the afternoon working. While I didn't have any home inspections to complete this week, I could still update a few reports as well as answer follow-up questions. I accepted a few new assignments and scheduled inspections for the next week. My responsibilities didn't stop because my life was in free fall. I spent the rest of my day until nightfall distracting myself with work and getting ahead on everything I had on my plate as a small business owner. It was good to have something to hold my focus; otherwise, I would have spent the time spiraling over all the unknowns.

Five minutes to sunset, Izzy arrived. She knocked on the door and let herself in. I locked up my office for the night and led Izzy to my car. It was still parked across the street from the adoption agency. With how packed the streets of Point Pleasant could get during business hours, it wasn't uncommon for people to park more than a block away from their intended location. I got into the driver's seat, and she claimed the passenger seat next to me.

"What's the plan?" Izzy asked.

I fidgeted with the door handle. "We have to see if anyone's in there first then sneak in and find the right records. Hopefully."

"All right." She leaned forward, studying the building. "Some lights are on, but I don't see any movement. There could always be someone hanging out at their desk, right?"

I nodded. "This may sound like a strange question, but how comfortable are your clothes?"

Izzy looked down at herself. She was dressed in a pair of yoga pants with a loose band T-shirt. When she was working as a reporter, she normally wore skirts with blouses and fashionable blazers. What she had on looked comfortable to me, but I wanted to make sure before I taught her the spell to heighten her senses. I could still clearly remember when I cast it while wearing a sweater that had a small piece of plastic from the tag still attached. It was something I barely noticed on a normal day, but with heightened senses, it had been almost unbearable.

"They're soft?" She raised her eyebrow.

I grabbed my notebook and jotted down the words to the spell. "This spell heightens your senses. I recommend closing your eyes, or it can get a bit overwhelming because everything heightens at once. You can dampen the sensations and focus in on one sense once the spell is in place, but the first few seconds can be a bit intense. I'll focus on my sense of hearing. I would suggest you focus on your sense of sight. If someone's in that building, one of us should be able to sense it."

Izzy swallowed and grabbed a stick of gum from her purse.

"What are you doing?"

Izzy popped the piece of gum into her mouth and chewed. "If my sense of taste is going to be heightened, I don't want to taste the burrito I had for lunch. It wasn't that good the first time."

I chuckled and gave her a minute to reset her taste buds. She spit the gum into its wrapper and slipped it into a small ziplock trash bag in her purse.

"Okay. I'm ready."

I closed my eyes and murmured the words to the spell that would heighten my senses. Izzy's voice lagged half a second after mine. Behind my closed eyelids, I could see the pulse of golden light. It was intermixed with a soft blue glow as well. As the last words of the spell exited my mouth, everything ratcheted up to eleven. I had purposefully changed out my entire wardrobe over the past year to only include soft-seam clothing. Fortunately for me, it seemed Kim had similar taste. The dress was soft and comfortable against my skin. My breath hitched at the strong scent of mint in the car. One by one, I dampened my senses until only my heightened sense of hearing remained. I opened my eyes and rolled down the window.

To a normal person's ears, the street would have been quiet. But I could hear the steady drip of water from a leaky faucet down the block. The crunch of tires on asphalt from two streets over echoed in my ears. I cocked my head, directing my attention to the business across the street. Next to me, Izzy inhaled deeply and held it. I followed suit and listened. I blocked out all the other sounds until I was focused only on the adoption agency. The fluorescent lights hummed with electricity, and the metal fire escape creaked as wind blew past. I sorted through the sounds coming from the building. Nothing sounded like a person. I exhaled sharply and released the spell. I tapped on Izzy's leg to encourage her to do the same.

The blue glow dissipated from her skin. She turned to me, wide-eyed. "That was amazing." With shaking fingers, she held the page out to me.

"Keep it," I said.

Her smile widened, and she slid it into her purse. It was her first written spell.

I rolled my window back up and fished out two protein bars from my purse, handing one to Izzy.

She eyed it before accepting it. "What's this for?"

"Magic takes energy. It's best to eat in case we need to cast another spell inside." I munched on my bar before getting out of the car.

Izzy followed suit and scampered after me as I trudged across the street to the front door. I tested the handle, but it was locked. I glanced down at the electronic pad with a code instead of a standard lock. I groaned. I might be able to figure out the numbers through my divination abilities, but figuring out the exact order might be more difficult. "You don't happen to be good at cracking electronics, do you?"

Izzy shook her head. "I can pick a lock—don't ask—but not one like this."

I stepped back from the door and checked my surroundings. The street was still empty. I hadn't heard anyone nearby when I'd checked. I shoved my hands into my pockets to calm my nerves and walked around to the side of the building. I stared up at the fire escape.

"There's no way I can reach that," Izzy said.

The bottom of the ladder was six feet up. She might have been able to reach it, but unless she had the strength to pull herself up by her arms alone, she wouldn't be able to tackle it without help. I chewed on my nails and studied the windows along the ground floor. They were all higher up on the wall with bars over them. The windows for the upper floors were wider, without the added security. The fire escape looked like our only option in.

"I'll give you a boost." I stepped up under the fire escape and linked my fingers together to form a stirrup.

Izzy looked between me and the fire escape. "And how are you getting up there?"

"Just trust me. I'll give you a boost." I widened my stance to brace myself.

Izzy shrugged and stepped next to me. She put her hand on my shoulder for balance and, in one smooth move, reached with her other hand, while her foot rose to my outstretched hands. I grunted with the effort of lifting her. She scrambled up, moving her foot from my hands to my shoulder then up to the lowest rung. She climbed a few more feet before she paused and looked down at me. "Now what?"

"Now I follow." I took a few steps back and sprinted forward, jumping up at the last second to grab the bottom rung. I used my momentum to swing forward, curling my midsection up and around the bottom rung. As I swung backward, I loosened my grip with my right hand and reached up for the next rung on the ladder. My legs swung backward, and I raised them, tucking my feet into the bottom rung. Then I sprang up and grabbed onto the next rung with my left hand before I lost my balance. I paused like that, curved, almost in the fetal position, with my feet on the lowest rung and my hands gripping the one above it. Once I was confident I wouldn't fall, I straightened and reached up for a higher rung. I quickly climbed until my head was just under Izzy's feet.

Izzy gaped at me. "What—How—Are you like Superwoman or something? That was some sort of insane gymnastic move."

I flushed. All my days at the gym were paying off. That, plus a few classes I had taken over the past few months at a parkour park. "I work out."

Izzy continued up the ladder ahead of me. "You need to take me to whatever gym you're going to because I want to know how to do that."

"If you help me find what I'm looking for, it's a deal."

We climbed the rest of the way up to the second floor in

silence and crouched next to the window that led into the adoption agency. It was a simple slide window. The lock looked rusted open. On the other side of the glass, a wooden stick rested between the window frame and the wall. It was wedged in there to keep the window closed.

"Shoot," Izzy whispered. "Not something I can help with either."

I stared at the piece of wood and murmured the words to a spell under my breath. My motes of light swirled forward, wrapped around the wood, and lifted it to the side.

"I'm glad you're a good witch," Izzy said.

I glanced over at her. "What?"

"Imagine what you could do if you were using your powers for evil. But instead, you're running around, solving murders, and rescuing people. Superwoman wasn't too far off."

I ducked my head to hide the blush spreading across my face. "I'm just doing the right thing." I opened the window and slipped inside.

Izzy followed.

The space was even more crowded with boxes than it had been that morning. The remainder of the files had been boxed up. They were stacked haphazardly around us. Each box was labeled with a range of last names, but because of how the boxes had been stacked, they were no longer in alphabetical order. Plus I didn't know if it was sorted by the last name of the adopted child or if it was by the last name of the parents who gave them up. Or something else. It was impossible to tell. I stepped farther into the room.

Izzy trailed her fingers on the set of boxes next to me. "I'll keep watch while you search?"

I nodded and moved deeper into the room once more. I knew what I was looking for, but I didn't know where it would be, so I closed my eyes and brought my magic to the surface. A few times in the past, my divination abilities had led me to useful evidence. When I moved closer to it, my body would react. I focused on how my body felt, particularly on the pulse of pressure at the back of my skull and the hair on my arms and neck. I inched through the room, my hands out at my sides.

It was slow going, taking almost ten minutes of moving one small step after another before anything changed. The hairs along my left arm rose subtly. I turned toward the sensation and moved forward a little. Another five minutes, and I had found the box my divination powers were reacting so strongly to. The hair on my arms and neck stood straight up, and the pressure at the back of my head pulsed so strongly I had to fight back a wince. I picked up the box. In a tight, blocky script were the words *Elliott, Lindsey - Emery, Matilda*. With shaking hands, I lifted the lid.

Some of the files were older than others, the pages yellowed with age. A few looked fresh. Halfway through the box was the file I was looking for: Ellison, Raymond. I pulled it out and flipped it open. My eyes scanned the pages. My heart skipped a beat when I reached what I was searching for. It was worse than I could have expected. My palms became sweaty. My whole body shook as I reread the names again and again. It wasn't a mistake. Raymond's father was Benjamin Hayes, one of the five men responsible for sending Meredith over the edge and onto her quest for vengeance. Raymond was a descendant.

"What is it?" Izzy asked.

I grabbed my phone and snapped a photo of the page before handing it to her.

"Oh." She stared at it with the same wide-eyed expression I wore. "How many more are there?"

"I don't know." I put his file back in his box and restacked everything the way I had found it so no one would be able to tell it had been disturbed. "It might be a coincidence. Maybe? Let's check to see if the first victim, Jennifer Moore, has a file in here too."

Izzy nodded, and we split up to cover more ground. I read through label after label. Now that we knew how the boxes were sorted, it was easier to find what we were looking for by reading labels than by me stumbling around, relying on my divination powers. I moved to the right, while Izzy went left. Using my phone as a flashlight, I read through label after label. I paused when I found the box marked *Morgan, Gregory - Morris, Rachel.*

"I think I found it." I quickly opened the box and searched through the files until I found Moore, Jennifer, near the front. I pulled it out and flipped it open. I found the information faster this time and closed my eyes after reading the father's name. She was another child of Benjamin Hayes. He had owned the local paper and was famous for being a bachelor. But it looked like he had more corpses in his closet than just the business with Meredith.

I snapped a photo of the page and slipped it back into place. I turned and searched for Izzy in the darkness. She stood hunched over a box on the other side of the room. Her shoulders shook, and all the color had drained from her face. Her mouth opened and closed without a sound.

"Izzy?" I whispered.

She shook her head and closed her eyes.

"Izzy?"

I came to a stop by her side. Wordlessly, she handed me the file in her hands. It was for a man named David Snowden. My eyes traveled down to the names of the birth parents. A lump formed in my throat. Somehow, it had gotten even worse. David Snowden was the child of Harold Mitchell and Meredith Walker.

"Oh god. We have to find this guy. He could have family."

Izzy shook her head. "We don't."

"What?" My head jerked toward her.

"David's my grandfather."

Time seemed to stop as reality caught up to me. "Izzy—"

"I'm one of the descendants too."

CHAPTER 19

Izzy didn't say another word at the agency. I had carefully boxed everything up and done another walk-through with my divination powers to make sure no other secret descendants had gone through the agency. We didn't find another name. Before we left, I double-checked that everything was exactly as we had found it. Then we exited the way we came in.

Izzy was wordless when we got back to Kimberly's house. She walked rigidly, her face forward, but her eyes were glazed like she couldn't see the walkway before her. I could only begin to imagine how hard it must be. While I had experienced the strain of discovering I was a witch from a cursed coven, her revelation took that further. She was descended from the witch responsible and the true villain in this story, the man who had started it all: Harold Mitchell. Her great-grandfather was a murderer. I kept pace with her as we trudged up the steps, trying not to rush her to the door.

I knocked and let myself inside. We walked past the guys in the living room playing an animated game of Go Fish and slipped into the kitchen, where the rest of my coven,

Kimberly, and my mother were hard at work preparing for the second attempt at banishing Meredith. I stepped in front of Izzy, hiding her from view as we stopped in the doorway. All eyes turned to me.

Megan smiled. "Great news. We think we might actually get our prep work done in time. We can try again tonight."

I pressed my lips together. "Lori, could you tell me about your visions again?"

She stiffened in her seat, studying my face, her brow furrowing. "Something happened."

I forced my expression to stay as neutral as possible. I didn't want my mother to get off track. "Humor me. Can you go over your vision again?"

"All of it?" Lori asked.

I bit the inside of my cheek to keep my face impassive. The entire drive over, I had replayed in my head all the conversations I'd had involving the curse. I was hoping I had misremembered what my mother had said about the necessary participants. If I was, then I wouldn't need to shine the spotlight on Izzy tonight. But if I wasn't… I closed my eyes. I didn't want to think about it. "Why don't you start with who needs to be involved?"

"Okay. A descendant of each of the witches present at the time the curse was cast needs to—"

"Each of the witches?" I asked.

"Yes." Lori frowned.

"Even Meredith?"

"It's a moot point. She didn't have any children."

The next words were heavy in my throat. I had to force them out. "What if she did?"

Lori blinked at me. She leaned back in her seat, a finger tapping her chin as she thought through the problem. "They would have to be there too."

I sighed and looked behind me. I held Izzy's eyes. It was her secret to tell, but it had to be told if we wanted to stop this. She nodded, giving me permission. It felt like my feet weighed a hundred pounds as I walked into the room and opened the picture of David Snowden's adoption paperwork on my phone. I dropped it on the table and pushed it toward Lori.

Lori swallowed. Her hands shook as she reached forward and picked it up. Her eyes darted between my face and the phone. "He's a boy. It doesn't mean—"

"It does." The words were like ash in my mouth.

"He had a daughter?" Lori asked.

"Another son, actually." Izzy inched into the room next to me. "But that son had a daughter. Me."

With that word, a collective inhalation rippled throughout the kitchen. All eyes zeroed in on the newest witch in the room as all the expectations, hopes, and dreams of an entire coven settled onto her shoulders. I squeezed her arm in support.

She gave me a weak smile and straightened under their scrutiny. "I guess I have a new ritual to learn, then, don't I?"

Megan exhaled sharply. "And we have another position in the circle we need to prepare for."

"That'll take all night," Betty said.

Sarah nodded. "If we start now, we might have it prepped before sunrise."

Agnes reached for a mortar and pestle and got to work. "And if not, we still have tomorrow night. This will work."

"Can I do anything to help?" Izzy asked.

Megan scooted her chair closer to Izzy and pulled out a sheet of paper. "This spell's a lot more complicated than anything you've worked on so far. I'll explain the high-level stuff, then we should practice funneling magic into each other."

I smiled and leaned against the doorway. I had dreaded coming into this room. It had felt like I was about to drop a bomb on all their hours of effort. But instead of fretting, they got to work. My gaze bounced from face to face. *This will work.* My eyes landed on my mother's face, and my smile faltered. She sat stiffly in her seat, her eyes wide and staring blindly forward. As if she could sense me watching her, she surged to her feet and bolted.

"Lori?" Agnes stared after her.

I pushed myself away from the door and followed. "I got it."

Lori hadn't gone far. She stumbled through the sliding glass door and knelt in the backyard, her fingers digging into the dirt.

"Sorry for dropping that on you, but… please? Could you hold it together for one more day?" I stopped in front of her. My heart lurched at the sight of her face. The despair rolling off her hit me like a freight train. I stumbled back, my eyes watering and my mouth dry in an instant. "Mom?"

"I'll never be able to make up for it, will I?" She continued clawing blindly at the earth. "I thought I was doing the right thing, you know? I really thought I was. And… and I can never, ever make up for it."

"What are you talking about?"

"I live so much of my life in the future. I can't keep it all straight. Things happen out of order. But I tried. I really tried. I've spent the last twenty years trying to get it straight this time, trying to fix it. But even now, it's jumbled, and no matter what I do, I can't catch the threads."

I knelt in front of her and put my hand on hers.

"That morning…" Her voice dropped to a whisper. She was so quiet, I had to lean in to hear her. "It was the worst morning of my life. The threads were spiraling. Everything was so disjointed. One second, I saw Grace come into her powers at six years old. She didn't survive it. It broke you. The next, I was standing in a circle with Megan and Kim. Meredith was there, and we were banishing her. Then Grace was thirteen years old and coming into her powers. She didn't survive it. It broke you. And I was back in that circle, still banishing Meredith. Then Grace was fourteen and dying. Then seventeen and dying… I couldn't stop it. Every time, she inched older and older. Every time, she died. Every time, it broke you. But between those flashes, I was with Megan and Kim. We were banishing Meredith. I heard the words. I heard them. I saw the ritual. I thought… I thought I knew what to do."

Tears streamed down her face. Her emotions battered against me. I struggled to find my own in the torrent of her despair. The thought that had plagued me for twenty years swam to the surface and slipped past my lips. "Then why'd you leave?"

Lori folded in on herself. "I saw you coming home and holding her. I saw it. I saw her in your arms. And the threads were spiraling. Nothing made sense. I thought you were home. I thought you came back. I thought she was safe and I could go do what needed to be done." She collapsed into my arms and wailed. "I'm so sorry. I couldn't keep the lines straight. I didn't know. I didn't know I had left her alone until after I failed to banish Meredith the first time, until after I was sitting in the hospital with Kim and saw your messages. But what could I say to you? You didn't know magic was real. You didn't know anything. And I still couldn't get the threads straight."

"That explains twenty years ago." Betty's voice cracked in anger.

I hadn't heard her come out. I turned my head and watched her stalk out of the house toward us.

"But what about all the other times before that? What about all the times you took off without notice?"

Lori shuddered and covered her face. "Please stop… This… this is between me and my daughter."

"No, it isn't. This is about all the times *I* had to clean up your mess." Betty strode around us, hitting her hand against her chest as she came to a stop in front of us. "Your mom, Mel, ran herself ragged trying to pay her bills and most of yours. She wasn't the one who had to pick Dani up from the train station in the middle of the workday. *I* did that. *I* was the one who had to explain to your daughter that she was good enough. That *your* taking off again wasn't a reflection on *her*. So what about all those times? What about every time you chose seeing the future over everyone else?"

"Is that what you think I did?" Lori whispered.

"It's what you always do." Betty towered over her. "You've always been the selfish one, Lori. Mel bound Dani's powers. She always could have done the same for you, but you didn't want her to."

"That was the hardest decision I've ever made." Lori closed her eyes, tears still streaming down her face. "Mel was more than just a once-in-a-generation witch. She was unique. When we figured out that she could bind powers by herself, without a coven backing her up, I begged her to do it to Dani. I begged again for Grace when I saw what would happen to her. But I couldn't beg for me, because I saw… I saw what would happen if I did."

"What did you see?" I asked.

Lori squeezed her eyes tighter. "That the binding would break with her death. Grace would still die. You would still break."

"Grace didn't die, though." I wrapped my arm around her shoulders. "She's still here."

"For now," Lori sobbed. "In my dreams, she dies at twenty-four, after giving birth to a beautiful daughter. And that daughter… that daughter dies too. You might like to think of me as selfish. But I chose seeing the future, I chose magic over a relationship with my own daughter, because if I didn't, all the future generations would suffer. They would all break. I had to see to stop that from happening. I had to see to make things right. At least that's what I thought. I thought I could save everyone."

Betty hovered over us. She opened and closed her mouth, trying to find the right words. After almost a full minute of watching Lori cry, she reached out, squeezed Lori's shoulder in a sign of forgiveness, and returned to the house.

Lori convulsed in my arms and clung to me as sobs racked her body. She mumbled the same words over and over. "I thought I could save everyone."

I held her while she cried, patting her hair. All the hatred I held against her unraveled inside me. "It'll be okay."

"But it's been hopeless this entire time. It didn't matter if I got the words right back then. It didn't matter at all because we didn't have all the pieces. And even now, after everything I've seen, I couldn't get things to line up straight in my head. I couldn't see that the puzzle wasn't complete. I'm failing. And I'll never be able to make it up to you. I'll never be able to make it up to anyone."

I pulled her onto her knees and held onto her. "You're not failing. Without you, we wouldn't have any hope at all."

She buried her head into my shoulder, her tears staining my dress.

I stroked her back. "It's going to be okay." And this time, when I said it, I didn't just mean the curse. I didn't just mean tonight. I meant us. I never thought I could forgive my mother for abandoning my daughter all those years ago. But in this moment, I saw hope that our relationship could mend and that everything would be all right. "You're the reason we're going to succeed."

Lori sniffled against me, her body relaxing. She leaned back and wiped at her face. "You go on ahead. I just need a minute to collect my thoughts."

"Are you sure?"

She nodded. "It's been an emotional day."

"I… I love you, Mom."

She blinked at me. Surprise morphed into happiness as she wiped another tear from her eye. "I love you, too, sweetheart." She smiled at me weakly. "I'll be right in. I promise."

I stood and walked back into the house. We still had a lot of preparations to do. But soon, we would be on the other side of this. And I had a lot to look forward to.

CHAPTER 20

I startled awake with someone's hand pressed to my shoulder. Chris still slept behind me, his arm flung over my waist, his head nestled against my back. I squinted into the darkened room until the shape above me took form.

"Mom?" My lips were chapped from sleeping in a dry room.

Lori pressed a finger to her lips. "Edith Voss has arrived. You need to get up."

I wiped sleep from my eyes and disentangled myself from the nest of blankets on the floor. I shivered against the chilly air—Kim liked to blast her AC at night—and trudged after my mother. The sky was still dark. I couldn't tell what time it was, but the entire house was still asleep. Bob snored away on the couch. Megan had passed out at the kitchen table, her face resting in a puddle of drool. Lori led me past her to the sliding glass door. We slipped out into the yard.

A woman stood a few feet from the back door. Head tilted back, she closed her eyes as she basked under the full moon. She was an imposing figure, standing just under six feet tall with a muscular build and wide shoulders that appeared even wider with her hands clasped at the base of her spine. Her short-cropped hair had flecks of white at the temples. I took her all in. She wore a long-sleeved gray Henley shirt and black slacks.

"I'll let you guys talk." Lori took a step back. "I'll be in the house if you need me."

Edith turned toward me, her storm-blue eyes calculating. "Miss Williams. Lori has already provided me with a statement, but it is best practice to get them from more than one source. For my own edification, please state your name and explain how the known criminal Meredith Walker managed to escape." Her words were harsh but held no malice. She had a calm, even tone.

I swallowed as my mother disappeared back inside the house. "Where would you like me to start?"

She didn't move at all. Her eyes didn't narrow. She just stood, taking me in. "That's for you to decide."

I tried to hold myself as still as she was, but it was hard to fight the urge to squirm under her gaze. "Well, um... I had recently arrived home. I was on my way to talk to my daughter about my engagement—"

"Please keep the personal details at a minimum; otherwise, we will be here all morning."

I winced and did what she asked. I cut out everything about how I felt and stated it all like a list of facts. We were in the kitchen; we felt the earth shake, and when we exited the house, the sky was green. I went through every detail, but when I reached the part where I visited Emily Park in the hospital, she raised her hand to cut me off.

"There was a witness?" she asked.

"Yes, she—"

"Then, let's go talk to her." Edith turned on her heel and walked toward the side of the house.

I chased after her. "She's still unconscious."

Edith didn't turn around as she kept walking. "And?"

"Sleeping people can't talk," I said.

"Not true." Edith continued on her way.

I trailed after her. She walked to a white Honda Civic, and without stopping, she climbed into the car. She turned on the engine and waited for me to get in. I scampered around the car and claimed the front passenger seat.

"Continue with your statement." Edith put the car into drive and stared straight ahead as we made our way through town. As we drove, I finished telling her about the other bodies and the failed attempt at putting Meredith to rest. The only shift in her expression was when I mentioned Miranda hadn't answered her phone. It was subtle, just a twitch of her eyebrow, but she remained wordless through it all. Somehow, I felt compelled to spill it all. I even revealed Izzy's secret.

She parked in front of the hospital, as it was still dark. The clock on her dashboard said it was three a.m. I didn't know if it was right or not. I hadn't checked my phone. She got out and strode toward the hospital. I trailed after her. She walked through the place like she owned it, every movement confident. She paused momentarily at the nurses' station to ask for Emily Park's room. Surprisingly, the nurse told her without a single question about why we were here or any reminder about visiting hours. I stared slack-jawed at the nurse as a silver shimmer sank into the woman's skin, and she turned back to her computer station as if nothing had happened.

Edith continued down the hallway and stepped into Emily's room without knocking. I scampered after her and slipped into the room only a few steps behind her. When I'd come with Chris, I hadn't gotten a good look at Emily. I remembered her appearing small in her bed. She still looked like she was sleeping. Her hair was braided to keep it from tangling. Her breathing was shallow but even. By her bedside, with his head tilted back against the back of the chair, was her husband. He took up all the free space in the room, his long legs splayed in front of him. The same silver sheen from the nurses' station slid up the sides of the chair and settled over his eyes and ears.

"What is that?" I whispered, pointing at the silver.

Edith cocked her eyebrow. "Magic doesn't require words so long as your intention is clear enough and the effect isn't complicated. A little extra grogginess isn't too difficult. So long as we're relatively quiet, he should stay asleep."

I peered down at him and relaxed my gaze to get a closer look at the spell she had used. I yawned and rocked forward on my toes, almost stumbling over his leg.

"Pay attention." Edith strode around the bed and stopped on the other side of it, farthest from the door. She held her hands out over Emily and closed her eyes.

"What are you doing?" I whispered.

"Checking to see if she's under the effects of a sleeping spell."

"What?" I gasped, looking back at Emily as I steadied my breathing and relaxed my eyes.

The shadows in the room deepened, and the whiteness of the sheets became stark in the dim room.

Edith murmured under her breath. My gaze darted to her hands. What looked like liquid mercury dripped from her fingers, spinning through the air instead of dropping straight down. It settled over Emily's temples and sank into her skin. I stumbled back from the bed as Emily jerked awake, her hand grasping for her chest as a scream erupted from her lips.

Her husband vaulted out of his seat, his eyes wide. He surged forward and grabbed Emily's hand. "Honey?" He pushed her hair to the side and cupped her chin. "Oh my god, you're awake. Doctor!"

A nurse burst into the room a second later. She looked between me, Emily, Edith, and the husband before springing into action to check Emily's vitals. Edith stepped back and watched like a hawk while they went through the motions of checking her pupils' responsiveness and asking simple questions like did she remember her name. Emily responded to each of them, her hands clenching and unclenching around the blanket twisted in her grasp. I pressed myself against the wall closest to the door and watched as a silver sheen spread across the floor from where Edith stood. The silver climbed up the husband's and nurse's legs. Once it reached the nurse's head, she stopped, glancing at Edith and me, then just focused on the questions.

Satisfied that Emily was stable, the nurse left to get the doctor. I stared after her as she disappeared down the hallway. *What the heck? Are we invisible?* When I turned back to Emily, it was stranger still. The husband sat on the side of the bed, his hand moving up and down Emily's arm in a show of comfort. The only one looking at me was Emily. Her eyes bounced between me, her husband, and Edith looming over her to the side. I could see the panic bubbling at the surface again the longer the silence held.

I stepped forward and grabbed a glass from the side table. Filling it with water, I then murmured a spell that would turn it into a relaxation potion. It glowed in my hands as I handed it off to Emily. "Drink this."

Her husband jerked as he stared at me as if seeing me for the first time. The silver sheen shifted over his skin, and he turned back to his wife with a tight smile. Emily slowly raised the cup to her lips. The first sip was hesitant, but then she downed the whole glass in a few seconds.

Her husband chuckled and took the glass from her. "We should probably make sure it's okay for you to drink more before I get you a second one, okay?"

She nodded and looked back at me. "Who are you?"

I glanced at Edith. Her eyes were closed, her lips pressed together in concentration. I didn't know if she could ask questions while maintaining the spell she had cast over the room. I inched forward. "My name's Dani Williams. I'm sorry to press you for information so quickly, but you witnessed something, and I need to know what you saw."

Emily wet her lips and settled back against her bed. Her eyelids fluttered as she leaned against her pillow, her skin glowing gold from the effects of my spell. "I was taking out the trash. I heard something. I thought it was a raccoon. I've seen it scavenging around the neighborhood. It's really cute, you know? They have such adorable little hands. I thought I might be able to get a picture of it, so I tiptoed around the side of my home. But the raccoon wasn't there.

"Instead, I saw this woman going into a house across the street. The abandoned one? I couldn't help myself. I've never seen anyone go inside before. I was curious, so I tried to wave, but she didn't see me. I started to walk over. She had left the front door open. I thought maybe I should introduce myself. I don't know why. It was late. It would have been rude, but… it was just all so strange. She was strange—her white hair, that blue dress. There were candles on the floor. I raised my hand—" Emily held up her hand in a fist, her knuckles pointed toward her face. She squeezed her eyes together, the first signs of distress eating at the edges of my relaxation spell. "When darkness erupted out of her. I felt something wrap itself around my ankle. Then I was here."

My mouth went dry. *The darkness is coming. White hair. Something wrapping around her ankle.* "That thing around your ankle, was it like a tentacle?"

Emily opened her eyes and frowned. "Yeah. It was. How'd you know?"

Dots connected in my head, dots I did not want to connect—my mother's warning and the image of Delaney Thornhill in Chris's living room when we first met. *It's a coincidence. Isn't it?* I backed out of the room, my hands sweaty.

"What is it?" Edith asked as she followed me.

"Is it common for two people's magic to look alike?"

"No." Edith stepped in front of me. She studied me. "Why do you ask?"

"What Emily described—it sounds just like Delaney's magic," I said.

Edith scoffed. "I was her partner for years. I know what her magic looks like."

"Black tentacles?" I raised my eyebrow.

Her brow furrowed. "Orange tentacles."

"No." I crossed my arms over my chest. "They're black."

Without warning, Edith grabbed the sides of my head. My vision blurred until all I could see were her storm-blue eyes. A silver sheen coated my vision, making her eyes appear to glow. I fought against her grasp. It reminded me of how Miranda had held me and forced a promise out of me. But instead of asking any questions, she just stared. My mind went blank as images flitted through it—memories of my encounters with Delaney, like snapshots from each encounter. The snapshots moved backward from the last time I had seen her, through Harold's capture, and finally to her intimidating entrance into my life when she broke into Chris's home in the middle of the night to scare me. The last image in my head was of her black tentacles holding me in place.

Edith dropped my face, her eyes wide. Her calm facade broke as she began cursing under her breath.

"What is it?" I asked.

Edith held my gaze. For half a second, I could see the fear in her eyes before her mask slipped back into place. "The only thing that can change how a witch's magic looks after their powers have settled is the influence of an Outsider."

I held my breath, waiting for the next sentence.

"It seems my former partner made a deal—and is probably here to make another one."

CHAPTER 21

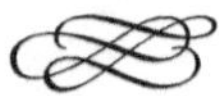

We drove back to Kim's house in silence. I peered at Edith from the corner of my eye. She sat like there was a steel rod up her back, her posture rigid and tense. Her hands gripped the steering wheel, her jaw clenching subtly. Her expression, though, was impassive, and the emotions I sensed in the car were muted, like everything inside her was under lock and key. Without a word, we parked across the street from Kim's house and trudged up the steps to the front door.

Lori sat on the step, her elbows resting on her knees. She stood as we approached and wiped dust from her pant legs. "I didn't see you leave."

I swallowed and stilled my hands. "We went to talk to the witness."

"And?"

Edith strode past her, pushing open the front door. "You should wake everyone up."

I followed her inside. It had been less than an hour since Lori had woken me from a dead sleep. So much had happened, so much had been revealed in our short field trip. It was hard to wrap my mind around it. I shook Chris awake and asked him to rouse the other men. He yawned and began making the rounds. Between him, me, and Lori, everyone was awake and standing in the living room within fifteen minutes, their eyes bleary, their hair rumpled from sleep. But despite the exhaustion clinging to them, they stared at me expectantly.

I gestured toward Edith. "This is Edith Voss, retired Warden of the West and, more importantly, Delaney Thornhill's former partner. We just got back from interviewing Emily Park, the witness who saw Meredith escape from her prison. Edith, could you please tell the group what you told me at the hospital?"

"I have reason to believe Delaney has gone rogue." Edith's voice was almost monotone, it was so flat. "It appears that she made a deal with an Outsider. And if my observations of others who have done the same are true, she is likely here to make another deal."

With each word, the unease in the room grew. Too many strong emotions swelled around me, holding me in place as confusion and fear warred for dominance. My eyes found Grace in the corner. She was shaking uncontrollably. I sent a mental nudge to Charlie, and he darted between the large group of people and pushed his body against her legs. She crouched and picked him up. Her shaking eased as he shoved his head under her ear and purred.

My gaze flicked back to Edith as she continued like she was reading from the phone book. "We need to act now, before she has more time to prepare. This is an all-hands-on-deck situation. We need to tackle all three at once if we want to succeed. If Delaney, Meredith, or the Outsider manage to escape, the issues will continue to compound."

Lori cleared her throat. "How are we supposed to lure Delaney here if—"

"The best place to take a stand is somewhere that resonates strongly with all three individuals. I would propose we make our attack at Meredith Walker's former abode before the sun rises in approximately two and a half hours."

"We've been prepping in the woods." Megan gestured to the greenbelt behind Kim's house. "It'll take time to move everything."

"Then I suggest you begin now." Edith's tone was harsh. It seemed, in her mind, it wasn't up for debate.

I studied the faces of those around me. The Retirees were clustered together, their hands gripping each other. Megan had her hand on Kim's shoulder as Kim leaned on her forearm crutches. Heather had her arm wrapped around Grace. Izzy hugged herself, but her eyes were fierce. Lori stared at her feet, muttering under her breath.

I tore my eyes from her face and studied the descendants —the innocent men we were trying to protect from something well outside what they should have been asked to understand. Bob was stoic, but his eyes were clearer than I had seen in days. Jay wore a frown, and Noah looked determined. Kevin stared at his son, his expression vacillating between fear and determination as well. He cared about Noah. He wouldn't be here if he didn't.

Finally, my eyes landed on Chris. He stared right back at me with trust in his eyes. I smiled weakly at him, and he closed the distance and pulled me into a one-armed hug.

I blinked away tears. This was too much. *How are we supposed to deal with all three at once?* My mind whirled as everything I knew about Meredith, Delaney, and the Outsider replayed in my head. The Outsider had said more than once that it would always come back. During our confrontation with Julie before Meredith escaped, it claimed it had made a promise and that it couldn't go home until that promise was complete. My heart stuttered in my chest. *Or until it's released by one of the Blood.*

My gaze landed on Izzy. Sticking our heads in the sand or running wasn't an option. Not anymore. We didn't really have a choice about fighting. But we had all the pieces we needed to win. "You heard the woman. Let's get a move on."

The witches strode for the back door.

Before Izzy could disappear after them, I grabbed her. "I need you to do something."

"Now?" she asked.

I shook my head. "After we banish Meredith." I grabbed a notebook and jotted down directions then shoved them into her hands. "When we're done banishing Meredith, read this."

I released her hands and turned toward the kitchen. The descendants stared at the assortment of potion vials and protection charms the Retirees had made with their assistance over the last twenty-four hours. They lay scattered across the counters.

I strode into the room. "Heather, we'll be using a lot of magic tonight. I need to make sure none of us falters because we're not properly fueled. Can you make sure every witch has something to eat? And preferably some coffee to help keep us focused?"

Heather nodded and darted toward the coffee pot to get it started.

"Noah and Jay, will you box up the potions? If you could put them in something that would make them quick to access, that would be great," I said.

Kevin cleared his throat. "I had a bunch of pouches same-day delivered. We can use those."

"Excellent." I stared at the charms on the counter. They were half done and still needed to be anointed and activated with magic.

"Where do you need me?" Bob stepped up next to me.

"Help me with these?" I gestured to the amulets. "I need to activate them, but if you could pour the protection oil onto them first and make sure everyone gets one, that would be great."

He nodded and reached for the protection oil. We worked

in tandem. He poured. I activated. He delivered the charm to someone who didn't have one yet. After my sixth charm, Heather shoved a muffin into my hands, and I quickly ate it before moving onto the next charm. While they wouldn't be able to protect us from any physical injury, they would protect us from mind control or possession—and when dealing with a vengeful ghost, that was a very real concern.

After the last charm had been activated, I quickly ate another muffin. As the group trickled back inside, Heather handed out the snacks and drinks before everyone piled into the cars. We drove as a small caravan from Kim's place to the neighborhood around Meredith Walker's house.

The street was still half blocked when we arrived. Large orange cones redirected traffic to one side of the street, away from the massive crack in the asphalt. There was no cloud cover in sight. The full moon filled the sky, blanketing the earth with its warm, pale glow. In the dim light, I could make out the edges of the crack. They seemed deeper and more cavernous at night. We clustered together on the sidewalk and stared up at the wreckage. The crumbled front half of the house hadn't changed since I was last there. The only difference was the orange caution tape that had been strung between the trees bordering the street, urging people away.

My breath hitched in my throat as movement from inside the house caught my eye. A white spot glided through the wreckage toward us. As Delaney stepped out of the ruined house, the moonlight caught on her hair. It was like a beacon in the night. She sauntered down the front steps, her hips swaying as she descended the uneven stairs. She faltered as Edith stepped up beside me. A smirk that had been forming at the corners of her mouth disappeared, replaced with a tight-lipped frown. She only paused for a second before she continued down the yard. Her movements shifted from languid to rigid and intentional.

"I didn't realize I had been sent back up," Delaney said.

"I've been tracking this coven for a while now. I'm almost done building my case against them. I don't think there's a law they haven't broken. Especially that one." She raised her finger and pointed directly at me. "Dani Williams of the Point Pleasant Coven, you are under arrest."

Bob stepped in front of me, blocking my view of Delaney. "My resignation letter hasn't been accepted yet, so I'm still the sheriff of this town. If anyone's going to make an arrest this evening, it will be me."

I opened my mouth. No words came out. *He's going to arrest me now? After everything I've done?* I gaped at him.

"While Miss Williams has been a nuisance since the day she arrived, meddling where she isn't—"

"By all means, arrest her, then." Delaney's voice was mocking as she cut him off.

I took a step back. Bob didn't turn around as he scoffed. "I do know the difference between someone trying to kill people and someone trying to save lives. And Miss Williams has done nothing but try to save lives since she arrived. Being a nuisance isn't a crime. So no, I think not. I refuse to *allow* her to be arrested today. Not by you or anyone else."

I froze.

"Get out of my way." Delaney's voice grew closer as she came maybe only a few feet away.

I poked my head out from behind my unexpected protector. Delaney stood inches away from Bob, her face twisted into a scowl.

Instead of her usual monotone, Edith's voice was pained. "Delaney. If you come willingly, the other Wardens might go easy on you."

"Easy on me? For trying to bring in criminals?" Her tone was sarcastic, but her voice shook on the last word, revealing her nerves.

"Cast a spell for me, Delaney," Edith said.

"Why?" Delaney took a step back.

"It's still orange, isn't it?" Edith took a step forward.

Delaney screamed, darkness erupting out of her as tentacles whipped out and battered us away. I stumbled as one hit my side.

Edith surged forward, and where the inky black tentacles touched her, they became coated in liquid silver. "Make the circle! Perform the ritual."

I scrambled away from her as she threw spells toward Delaney. Blackness and silver clashed. The ground shook as the trees along the street began to move. I turned away from it and forced myself to move toward my coven. During the confrontation with Delaney, they had backed up a few steps. A few pieces of white stone had already been placed on the ground when I stopped next to Kim. She muttered under her breath, creating a makeshift ward around us all while we worked.

As the battle between Delaney and Edith raged behind me, I focused on the task at hand. I moved robotically as I grabbed the next white rock from the duffel bag. We scurried around each other, building up a circle that was wide enough for all the witches to stand around. We worked quickly, trying not to bump into each other as the ground shook, and green lights joined the mix behind us. Nausea rolled through me as a familiar sensation seeped into the air around us.

I glanced behind me. Edith was still holding her own against Delaney, but it was an even match. Neither one had gained an inch as they threw spell after spell at each other. Green goo slid across the ground toward us, and in the darkness, I could make out shapes shuffling forward.

"Hurry!" I yelled.

Jay and Noah handed out fanny packs to all the nonwitches. The descendants, joined by Chris and Heather, spread out, standing between us and the chaos inching its way across the grass and onto the roadway.

My hands shook as I poured the purifying potion onto

the northernmost point. My eyes kept bouncing up to Heather and Chris. They were here because of me. I had pulled them into this. If they got hurt… I squeezed my eyes shut for a second and pushed the thoughts aside. *I don't have time to panic. Focus.*

Megan spread the purifying potion on the southernmost point as Betty covered the Eastern and Lori the Western. With that, the circle was done. I didn't stop to think. I just reached out and grabbed the hand closest to me. It was Kim. She didn't falter. She reached out to the other side, continuing the circle. Izzy slipped in next to me and grabbed my hand on the other side. We all shuffled forward a step until our toes were pressed against the rocks on the ground and the circle was as tight as it could get.

Lori started the chant, like she had last time. This time, we all knew the words. We joined in on the second sentence and poured our power into each other. Golden motes of light danced between oddly shaped pearls, floating red orbs, rose petals, flickering flames, and purple-and-silver sparkles inside a teal haze that hung over the space. Izzy's almost-water-like blue lights entered the circle last. They splashed along the ground and slid up the sides of the circle as if filling a glass.

The power in the circle pulsed as it grew stronger and stronger. The pressure in the back of my head seemed to ebb and flow with the beat. The words flowed from all our mouths with the same cadence. Once again, we had chosen a tune we could all follow easily. As the battle raged around us, we chanted our spell to the tune of "Twinkle, Twinkle, Little Star." If I weren't so scared, it would have been humorous.

Glass vials broke behind me as the men threw them at the dark figures I could feel approaching. With every step closer they drew, the queasier I felt until I had to close my eyes and focus every ounce of my will on the next words, the next sentence of the spell. I couldn't fail. I squeezed Kim's and Izzy's hands as I tried to ground myself in the moment.

"Traitors!"

I almost sagged with relief when Meredith's voice rang through the night, but we couldn't stop now. My eyes flew open, and we proceeded straight into the second spell without faltering.

Meredith beat against the edge of the circle. With every hit of her fist, she shouted that word again and again. "Traitors!" Her eyes brimmed with rage.

More glass vials broke behind me. Someone stepped closer. I could feel their heat on my back. More glass shattered as other potions flew.

"Traitors!"

My hands ached as I gripped Kim and Izzy. I pushed harder, throwing more of my will into the spell. By this point, I had handed my mother so much of my magic, it was almost being pulled out of me as fast as I was pushing it. I didn't know if either of us could stop it now. The power continued to grow and pulse, the lights almost blinding. I widened my stance as the ground heaved under us. The pressure inside my head was almost unbearable. I blinked back tears as I screamed the last word of the spell into the night.

The lights flickered and died.

My breath caught in my throat as Meredith shuddered and split into two forms. Meredith became more solid, her hair shifting from white to red. Her eyes stopped glowing, and she curled in on herself. The rage vanished in an instant, replaced with despair that ripped into me. I choked back a sob. My gaze flicked to the other form. I couldn't focus on it. It glowed green. Some features looked human, but my eyes couldn't focus on any one trait long enough for it to make an impression other than that this creature was wrong in some way.

Lori spoke first. "Booker's waiting for you on the other side."

I wet my lips as Meredith looked up, tears streaking down her face. "Harold was arrested. All the men responsible are either behind bars or dead."

The Retirees spoke as one. "It's okay. You can let go. It's time for you to rest."

Meredith shuddered. A sad smile spread across her lips, and she disappeared.

Izzy dropped my hand, and she fumbled for the piece of paper I had handed her before we came here. She quickly unfolded it and turned toward the Outsider. "As Meredith's blood relative, I release you from your promise."

The Outsider smiled. It was too wide, with too many teeth. Then it, too, was gone.

I stared blankly ahead at the empty circle.

Then another glass vial broke behind me. I spun toward Meredith's house. Edith and Delaney were still flinging spells back and forth. Sweat drenched Edith's face. Her arms shook as she hurled a fireball at Delaney's feet. Delaney caught it and spun it in a different direction before it exploded in the air. The shadowy forms that had been inching forward lay still on the ground, no longer puppeted by the Outsider. The men had inched forward and were preparing to toss the few remaining potions they had at the last target: Delaney.

I grabbed Izzy's hand and walked forward. Together, we poured our energy into Edith. Delaney stumbled and turned, trying to flee into the house. Edith chased her up the steps, tackling her as she stepped into what remained of the living room. She bucked as Edith wove a spell that created handcuffs out of pure magic around Delaney's wrists.

Edith grunted. "Delaney Thornhill, you are under arrest. Stop fighting."

Delaney continued to thrash. Edith pushed her harder into the ground until Delaney finally stilled. I pushed a bit more magic toward Edith, which she used to whisper a sleeping spell into Delaney's ear. Delaney passed out cold, her breathing slowing.

I sank to my knees in the street. My whole body ached. Exhaustion clawed at me, trying to lull me to sleep. "We did it," I murmured.

Izzy sank to the ground next to me. My entire coven collapsed as it hit us how much magic we had used. I reached into my pocket and pulled out a small snack I had squirreled away for after the fight. I broke off a piece of the chocolate bar and handed it down the line. We sat there, munching on chocolate, as the sun began to rise, and I realized, as I leaned back on my hands, that we were not alone. During the fight, half the street's residents had stumbled out of their homes to stare at us with wide eyes. Magic had come to Point Pleasant, and I wasn't sure we would be able to put the cat back in the bag.

CHAPTER 22

It had been weird around town for the last three days. Point Pleasant was swarming with Wardens of the West. Everywhere I looked, another pair strode down the street. While not all were obvious, it didn't take a genius to figure out what they were. They all had the same gaze that penetrated through me, and they radiated disapproval. On the other hand, no one around town was acting like anything had changed. No rumors had started about what went down outside Meredith Walker's house. It was like the Wardens had cast a spell over the entire town to make them stop asking questions. At least for now.

I stepped into Slice of Life diner. Cold air blasted onto my bare shoulders from the AC vent overhead. I glanced around the space. Just like the rest of town, a set of Wardens stood to the right of the counter, while the rest of the room seemed completely normal.

I found my group at the booth in the back. Heather, Megan, Grace, and Chris were crammed onto the bench seat, while Izzy, Lori, Kim, and the Retirees had pushed together two more tables to make everyone fit. The descendants had claimed yet another table adjacent to the group. Between everyone, we occupied almost a third of the restaurant. I'd had to work most of the morning, performing my first few home inspections in over a week, so I had arrived late to the party. The tables were littered with half-eaten plates of food and empty cups.

I waved at them before making a pit stop at the hostess stand to put in my order. Abby was behind the counter today. Her pixie cut had been touched up and was spiky around her ears. Before I could open my mouth, she held up her hand.

"Let me think. You look like you're in the mood *for*," she lengthened the word for a few seconds before continuing, "a grilled salmon burger with a fig-and-blackberry tart for dessert."

My mouth watered. I had been considering something else, but that sounded delicious. I nodded. "You know me so well."

Abby beamed and punched in the order. "Kelsey! Another salmon burger."

I blinked, my head darting between her and the kitchen. I caught a glimpse of Kelsey Harmon tossing a handmade salmon burger onto the grill top. "You gave her a job."

"Yeah. She's a good worker. I hope she can stay." She sighed. "But if her ex tracks her down, my dad is already working on a good exit strategy for her. We've got this."

I smiled at her. Abby really was great at helping people get their lives back on track. If her calling weren't already to be a chef, I could see her making a real difference with community work. *Maybe she can do both?* I shook my head and focused on why I was lingering at the counter. "I have another favor to ask."

"Oh?" Abby cocked her eyebrow.

"Chris and I are getting married. I was hoping you might be willing to—"

Willow burst out of the kitchen, her floral-print maxi dress billowing around her legs. "We'll do it."

My mouth fell open. "I—"

"We already have ideas for the menu. We've been brainstorming for days," Abby gushed.

I continued to gape. I had come to ask them to cater the wedding. *How did they know?*

Willow blushed. "The Retirees may have accidentally spilled the beans about the engagement. And we may have gotten a bit too excited thinking about food for your reception."

"So excited we may have also started creating a menu for the engagement party," Abby said.

I laughed. "I guess we'll need to set up a tasting day or something."

Willow nodded. "I'll message you to set something up."

"Oh, and, Dani?" Abby leaned her elbows on the counter. "Congratulations."

Smiling from ear to ear, I thanked them and disentangled myself from the conversation so the next person in line could put in their order. I made my way over to the back corner where everyone was gathered and slid in next to Chris. He held out his hand under the table, and I twined our fingers together.

I leaned in and whispered into his ear, "The catering is taken care of."

He smiled back at me. "Now we just need to figure out the venue."

I laid my head on his shoulder and turned my attention to the conversation at the table. Despite how large the group was, it felt so normal. Heather was discussing the latest batch of foster kittens that she had picked up that morning from the local vet's office. They had an agreement. A local group that helped trap, neuter, and release community cats would bring them to him. He would vet them, and if he got the impression they would do well in homes, he would contact Heather.

Last week, the group had trapped a very pregnant cat who had given birth at the clinic. Both the mom and her babies were holed up in the kitten room at Heather's cafe, waiting to be old enough for adoption. Star, Charlie's mom, had shoved her way into the room and was demanding to assist in the kitten care. She was the resident foster mom and had taken care of most of the cats that had come through Heather's doors. She was the one permanent resident, and I knew Heather would never put her up for adoption. She was too attached. Plus having a good social cat to help show the new arrivals the ropes made the process smooth. Heather had a high success rate at finding good homes for her fosters.

The bell over the front door jingled. I glanced toward it and froze. Standing in the doorway was a witch I hadn't seen since the showdown at Meredith's house: Miranda Blackwood. After we had arrested Delaney, we'd found Miranda inside the house under the effects of a sleep spell. According to Edith, Delaney didn't kill her because all Wardens have a spell hanging over them that sends an alert to their home office if that Warden is killed on the job. Delaney didn't want to deal with a slew of investigators coming into town to figure out the cause, so she put Miranda into a deep sleep instead.

She still looked a little worse for wear. Deep shadows surrounded her blue eyes. Her jet-black hair was pulled back into a loose ponytail. The black robe she wore hung limply from her form as she shuffled through the room. She came to a stop at our group of tables and peered down at me. A small spark shone in her eyes, showing me her fire wasn't out, just momentarily dimmed.

"How are you doing?" I asked.

Miranda pressed her lips into a thin frown before

clearing her throat. "I'm here to give you an update. I felt you deserved to know that Delaney Thornhill was found guilty this afternoon of making deals with Outsiders as well as for the murders of Jennifer Moore and Raymond Ellison."

I released a breath I hadn't realized I was holding. "Did she say why she did it?"

"She said that after Edith was hurt during their last mission together, she was looking for a way to get an edge against the rogue supernatural creatures we hunt. She thought she could make one deal then banish the creature, but… she had not anticipated how the deals can corrupt a witch so easily. The boost to her powers was like a rush she could not have prepared herself for. And she wanted to feel that again."

My jaw dropped at the words *supernatural creatures*. She said it so matter-of-factly that I didn't know how to interject without looking foolish. *What else is out there?* I opened and closed my mouth, trying to find something to say.

"What will happen to her now?" Megan asked.

My eyes bounced from Megan to Miranda.

"Delaney is being transferred to a maximum-security witch prison in Wyoming."

My eyes widened. "Witch prison? Those exist?"

Miranda gave me a small smile. "There's an entire witch society out there—not just prisons but universities too. Entire towns openly practice magic. But they are shrouded by Wardens, so only those in the know can get inside."

"How have I never heard of these things before?"

"You've been isolated out here." Miranda gestured around her. "But that's about to change."

"What do you—" I began.

"Because you helped take down Delaney, I feel I owe you all a heads-up. Due to so many locals becoming aware of magic in this town, the Council has decided to set up a

Warden of the West office here to contain the situation. I will be stationed here for the foreseeable future."

For the second time during the conversation, I was at a loss for words. I sat there, my mouth opening and closing as I struggled to formulate a sentence. Finally, I landed on, "Welcome to Point Pleasant."

"Now that Delaney is convicted, you are all free to go about your lives. I suggest you keep your noses clean because the Wardens will be watching." Miranda gave me a crisp nod then retreated from the table. She strode out of the diner with her head held high.

Silence descended over our group with her absence as we all sat and digested what she had told us. An entire witch society existed out there, a witch society that was now coming here. The Wardens weren't going anywhere. The entire town was about to change, and I didn't know if it was for the better or worse.

And yet, as I looked around the table, I couldn't help but be excited. Grace sat across from me without gloves on her hands. Megan chatted amiably with Chris, and no one gave her a second glance. The ugly rumors around town about her had stopped overnight. I slid my fingers along the edge of the table. All I felt was the wood. I hadn't activated my divination powers, so I didn't feel anybody's emotions when I touched it. Not unless I wanted to. It really felt like this was a new beginning. We all had clean slates and could choose what to do with our lives next.

Agnes was the first to stand. She stared longingly at the front door before looking down at her best friends Betty and Sarah. "I think it's time for us to take that road trip."

Betty grabbed her purse. "I've been eyeing RVs all week. I think I've found one in Edmonds we can afford."

"Good. I've already mapped out a path to California." Sarah followed suit. "We'll finally get to see the redwoods together."

The Retirees paused and turned toward the rest of us. My eyes misted over. With their curses broken, Agnes could leave Point Pleasant and explore the world. It was one of her secret longings, and now she got to do it. I couldn't be happier for her. But I would miss them. Everyone at the table stood and hugged them before they left. They walked out of the diner, arm in arm, and headed off to their next great adventure.

After that, the group began to break up.

Noah was the next to stand. "I've got to head out to pick up Lucy."

Grace cocked her head. "Who's Lucy?"

Noah smiled widely and pulled out his phone. "Only the bestest girl in the whole world." He flipped his phone around to show off a picture of a dog.

Grace grabbed the phone for a closer look. "She's beautiful!"

She handed the phone to me so I could take a peek at the picture. I grinned down at it. Lucy was a red-and-white pit bull with the brightest smile, her tongue lolling out of her mouth. She was wearing a bright-pink collar as she stared out at the camera with adoration in her eyes. I handed the phone off to the next person, and it quickly made it around the table, with everyone oohing and aahing over her adorable face.

"She's a rescue. She just turned two. She's super smart too. She just learned her seventeenth trick. I didn't want her in the middle of all this in case things got hairy, so she's been with the sitter for the past few days." Noah leaned over the table to snag his phone. He thrust it back into Grace's hands. "Give me your number so you can come to the park with us next week. She'll be more than happy to demonstrate all her tricks, with the proper food motivation, of course."

Grace typed her number into his phone and handed it back. "Sounds like a plan. Text me to set something up."

"Will do." Noah waved to the table and made a beeline for the door.

"Wait up!" Jay called after him. "Mind dropping me off at Roxanne's?"

Noah held the door for him. "You guys are still dating?"

Jay elbowed him on the way out. "Don't act surprised."

They disappeared outside.

Only a few seconds later, Bob stood. He rubbed the back of his neck with a sheepish expression. "Speaking of, I should probably head out too. I promised Peggy I would cook dinner for her, and I still need to stop by the store to pick up steaks."

My eyes widened. Peggy had worked at the sheriff's station with Bob for a few decades. She had been loyal to him for years. I had no idea it had taken a more romantic turn.

Bob stepped toward me and offered his hand. "Miss Williams, I never thought I would say this, but it was an honor working with you on my last case."

I shook his hand, then he left too.

I looked around at the remaining faces. Izzy was nodding along to something I couldn't hear, and Lori sat, fidgeting with her napkin.

I cleared my throat. "How about everyone else? What do you all have planned now?"

Izzy shrugged. "Nothing concrete yet. But I have some promises I need to keep."

"Like what?" I asked.

Izzy glanced to the side again. Ghosts still followed her wherever she went, but since the curse was broken, she had found it easier to block them out or send them away. Apparently, her inability to keep the ghosts away had been a curse as well. She smiled. "Bellamy's cat was adopted by a family up near Deception Pass. I promised I would take him there to check in on her. I have a feeling he just needs to see her safe, then he'll be able to pass on."

I nodded. "Good luck."

Izzy stood and left.

My gaze shifted to Lori. She continued to fidget with her napkin, tearing it into small pieces and piling them next to her plate.

"How about you?"

Lori looked down at her hands. "I hoped you would be open to me sticking around for a while. Maybe staying in the guest room for a few days until I can find an apartment to rent?"

I put my hand over hers. "I would like that."

Lori peered up at me through her hair. A small smile spread across her lips as she straightened. "Really?"

I nodded.

"Then I should probably go do some shopping. I only have a duffle bag full of stuff, and I really need to flesh out my wardrobe." Lori grinned and slid out of the booth. "I'll see you when I get home?"

"Sounds like a plan," I said.

"I'll come with you." Grace grabbed her bag. "I've missed being around people. Going to a mall sounds like a fun victory lap for me."

Lori had a spring in her step as they made their way toward the exit. It had been years since my mom had put down roots. Her staying here was a very big step. I chewed on my lip as she left. While I still wasn't over everything she had done, I understood and wanted to get to know her. I wanted to give her a chance to prove herself. If the last few days were any indication, she would. And Grace was intent on helping her prove it to me.

I turned to the few remaining people at the table—Megan, Kim, Heather, and Chris. "And then there were five."

"I, uh... don't have anywhere else I need to be right now," Kim said. "But next week, I have my first appointment with an orthopedic surgeon. The Wardens helped me find one who's a witch. With the curse lifted, my bones are finally healing. While I don't have any guarantees yet, I'm hopeful that I'll be able to walk without my crutches in a few months."

"That's great!" Megan grabbed Kim's hand. "I'm so happy for you."

"Did you want to come?" Kim asked Megan.

"Of course," Megan responded.

I glanced at Heather. She was doing her best to keep her face blank, but she couldn't keep the emotions out of her eyes. I fought the urge to check. Now that I had a choice, it felt like I was spying when I looked into what someone was feeling. Instead, I tackled it the old-fashioned way. I studied her. She wore a small smile, but her eyes watered. *Bittersweet happiness?*

I cleared my throat and caught her gaze. "How about you, Heather? Any plans?"

Heather pressed her lips together and shook her head. "You know me. Old reliable. I'll just keep running the cafe. I'm not going anywhere."

I reached out and squeezed her hand. "Are you okay?"

"I..." Heather looked around the table and blushed. "It'll sound stupid."

"Try me," I said.

She ducked her head. "Since the temporary coven dissolved, I've missed knowing how everyone is doing. I've missed feeling your presence in the back of my mind. It was more calming than I thought it would be."

"I'm not going anywhere either," Megan said.

I glanced between Heather, Megan, and Kim. All three glanced between each other, a hopeful expression growing. None of us were going anywhere, and we had all been through the wringer together. I squeezed Heather's hand again and reached across Chris to take Megan's. Megan instinctively reached for Kim, who in turn reached for Heather. We formed a small circle.

"Do you know what I'm thinking?" I asked.

"Yes," Megan said. "And I think it's a great idea."

"Someone want to fill me in?" Chris asked.

I dropped Megan's and Heather's hands and took Chris's under the table. "We're forming a coven."

"A permanent one this time," Megan said.

Heather clapped her hands. "We've got so much to plan. I loved the ritual we did last time, but this one has to be even better. I need to bake. We can't form a coven without the perfect cookie to seal the deal."

The other women leaned in and began throwing cookie ideas back and forth. It was quickly decided that the Bizzy Bean would still be the coven's headquarters. Kim suggested that we wait for the next full moon. Since a full moon had marked the end of the curse, it only felt appropriate for another full moon to mark the start of our new coven.

I nodded along for a while, my head resting on Chris's shoulder. After a few minutes, the table quieted as Abby dropped off my food and collected the plates. When Abby left, the conversation over baked goods continued. I threw in a few ideas between mouthfuls of salmon burger.

After a while, the conversation shifted toward other plans. Chris began to chime in more as the topic of conversation landed on our wedding.

"I've always wanted an outdoor wedding," Chris said.

I squeezed his hand. "So long as I have a very big tent to get ready in."

The conversation devolved into tent discussions, bell tent versus pavilion. I had a hard time choosing. They both had pros and cons. Kim, surprisingly, had strong opinions on the matter. In her mind, bell tents were superior based on appearance alone. They had more character.

As the conversation continued, I looked around the table.

At thirty-nine when I got divorced, I thought my life was starting over. At forty, when I discovered I was a witch, I thought the same thing. And now, at forty-one, the same thought crossed my mind again. Life was resetting. Change was coming, but right now, with Chris holding my hand under the table and good friends around me, life was good.

EPILOGUE

EIGHT MONTHS LATER

Butterflies had been flying around in my stomach all day. The makeup artist put the finishing touches to my lips and stepped back. Turning, I stared at myself in the mirror. My dark-brown hair hung in ringlets around my face, curled to perfection. A flower crown with a gossamer veil was pinned to my head. And my gray eyes appeared bigger than they ever had before. The makeup artist had worked wonders on my face. My gaze traveled down to my white gown. When I had divorced Ed, I never thought I would do this again. But here I was, a few minutes from walking down the aisle.

Lori ducked into the bell tent and moved up behind me. Her eyes glowed with pride as she stared at our reflections in the mirror. "Five-minute warning."

I swallowed my nerves and stood. My hands flew across my gown, smoothing things into place as we moved to our positions inside the tent. The bridal party stood to the left of the exit, and across the way, on the other side of the tent opening, the groomsmen gathered. We stood in silence, the energy buzzing around the space as my bridesmaids, Megan,

Kim, and Grace, straightened my train and rechecked the clips in my hair.

Lori stepped out of the bell tent and tied the flaps back so we could exit without ducking our heads. Through the opening, I could see the rows of people lining the grass, waiting for the wedding to begin. A hundred people, if not more, sat out there. It felt like the entire town was in the audience, waiting for *me*.

With my dress straight, my makeup perfect, and the seconds ticking by, we lined up in order along the sides of the tent so the guests couldn't see us if they looked back. The voices outside melded together into a gray noise. I gripped my bouquet in front of me, my palms sweaty. The music outside began, and Grace stepped forward. Harrison took his position at her side, and together, they stepped out of the tent and into the aisle. The sound of voices stopped, and a heavy sense of expectation hung in the air.

Kim was next. It had taken six months for her to heal, but now, she walked without crutches. She was met by Stephen Bishop, the town mayor. Over the past nine months, Chris had been working closely with Stephen as the acting sheriff, then the newly elected one. They had become fast friends. Stephen held out his arm for Kim, and they turned and exited the tent together.

Megan waited thirty seconds, then she stepped forward to her mark. She was joined by Victor. He smiled down at her and raised his hand to smooth a loose strand of her hair into place. She flushed and turned to the right. He moved with her, and they both disappeared from the tent. I shuffled forward as the group got smaller. After another thirty seconds, Heather stepped forward, meeting Bob in the middle. They turned together and exited the tent.

Charlie stood waiting at my feet, a ring box strapped to his back. He stared at the spot he was supposed to move to when it was time, his tail swishing behind him.

Lori stepped up in front of me and reached for my veil. "Thank you for letting me be here as a parent today. It means a lot to me that you asked me to walk you down the aisle." Lori's eyes brimmed with tears.

Her gaze was clear, her eyes focused on the here and now. Since we'd broken the curse, she had been more present and able to live in the moment. When I was growing up, those times had been sparse. I had cherished each and every one of them. And now, it was the norm. She was here, and she, for once in my life, was reliable. Lori lowered my veil in front of my face and stepped to the side.

I looped my arm through my mother's. "I wouldn't have it any other way."

Charlie exited the tent, walking down the aisle ahead of me. Oohs and aahs issued from the guests outside. Though big, he was an adorable cat. He still hadn't stopped growing despite reaching my knees. He was easily thirty pounds of fluff and muscle.

I took a steadying breath and counted. When I reached thirty, I stepped out of the tent with my mother on my arm. Together, we walked down the aisle toward Chris. He stood there at the end. My eyes found him immediately, and I stared at his face the entire way. It had been months since I'd opened my divination powers to experience what others felt. But with the joy coursing through my body, I opened that door inside myself. My face broke into the biggest smile as the happiness from him, my mother, and everyone gathered mingled with mine. My heart burst with delight as I took the last few steps toward my future.

Time passed in a blur of sensation and exuberance. The next thing I knew, I stood staring at the love of my life while Betty gave her introduction speech next to us. "There's a saying that 'good men finish last.' And let's be honest—people love to throw that one around like it's something negative that explains everything. But what most folks forget is that there's another saying: 'Good things come to those who wait.' If ever a couple proved both those things true, it's Chris and Dani."

I grinned like a fool as I stared up at him.

Betty continued next to us, her voice projecting over the crowd. "Now, some of you might say Chris is finishing last—after all, it took him over forty years to settle down. But let's not confuse timing with losing. Because what he's getting today? He's not just finishing the race—he's crossing that line with a prize worth waiting for. And Dani? Well, she's no slouch in the patience department either. She found someone who would see her clearly, love her fiercely, and stand beside her through thick, thin, and all the weird stuff this town throws at them—which, let's be real, is *a lot*."

The crowd chuckled.

"This isn't some whirlwind fairy-tale romance. This is the kind of love that grows roots. The kind that weathers storms, stubborn streaks, and small-town gossip. So, today, we're not just here to celebrate a wedding—we're celebrating the kind of love that takes its sweet time, shows up when it's ready, and sticks around for the long haul. And if you ask me, that's the best kind there is.

"Now, enough of me flapping my gums. Let's get to the part where we make this thing official, before either of them gets cold feet or something crazy interrupts us. I understand you've written your own vows? Dani, you're up first," Betty said.

My hand shook as Heather handed me a notecard on which I'd jotted down a few words to keep me focused. "Chris. When I came to Point Pleasant, I thought I was starting over on my own. I thought I was doomed to be alone. I didn't know I was starting *this*—this life, this love, this journey with you. From the moment I arrived, you've been beside me—sometimes as a partner in chaos, sometimes as the calm to my storm. But always there. Always steady, through every twist, every challenge, and every impossible moment. All of it led me to this. To you."

Chris's smile widened as he beamed at me.

I folded the paper and continued from memory. "You've shown me what it means to be patient. And patient doesn't mean just waiting. It means putting in the work when things get difficult. It means *truly* showing up—for the people you love, for your community, for me. But it's not your patience I love most. It's your kindness, your generosity, the way you always strive to do the right thing, even when it's hard—even when no one is watching."

Chris continued to hold my gaze. The love rolling off him in waves stole my breath away.

I swallowed past a lump in my throat as more happy tears appeared at the corners of my eyes. "You are a good man, Chris. Not just good to me but good at your core. And today, I feel so blessed—not just to be marrying the man I love but to be marrying a man I admire. Whatever comes next, I know we'll face it together. And I promise you, I will do my best to be as patient as you are as we go on the rest of this adventure together. I can't wait to spend the rest of my life with you."

The audience sniffled as I handed the notecard back to Heather.

Chris cleared his throat and held my gaze as he began his vows. He had been practicing them for days, so he didn't need notes to get them right. He reached out and took my hands in his. "Dani, I've known since I was fourteen that you were something special. You had just shown up in town, taking a bus all on your own, and you were both feisty and kind. I didn't know until a few years later that I loved you. I figured that one out when I was seventeen. And it just took me a little longer than I would've liked to get to this moment. We took detours—life, timing, a whole lot of stubbornness on both our parts. But I'd walk every mile of that winding road again if it led me right here."

My heart thumped hard at his words.

He reached forward and held my hands, his thumb brushing against my knuckles. "Because I love you, Dani Williams. I love your stubborn spirit—even when it drives me crazy. I love how you always try to help others, even with more on your plate than anyone could handle. I love your laugh, and I love your silent moments. I love the way you see people—*really* see them. You show up, again and again, without hesitation, because it's right and because that's who you are. You are my compass, my partner, my heart. I'm the luckiest man alive to be standing beside you today."

My hands were steady in his. Despite all the raw emotions, I had never been so sure of something in my life. This moment was everything. It was perfect. It was where I was meant to be.

He squeezed my hands, his gaze burrowing into my soul. "So, here's what I vow. I vow to help you carry the weight when the world tries to stack too much on your shoulders. I vow to love you fiercely and gently in equal measure. And I vow to make the small moments count—because with you, even the quiet mornings and the everyday chores feel like something extraordinary. I love you. I've loved you for most of my life. And I always will."

Betty dabbed at her eyes and cracked a few more jokes before leading us through the rest of the ceremony. Chris and I went through it, almost shouting *I do* after each of her sentences. In sickness and in health, in good times and in bad, we promised each other our lives and our love. Before I knew it, she was uttering the words "By the power vested in me by Washington State, I now pronounce you Mr. and Mrs. Harris."

Chris kissed me with passion, then we made our way back down the aisle. Time passed in a blur between photos, eating cake, and dancing together. Willow and Abby had outdone themselves on the menu. They even collaborated on the lemon cake. It leaned into the spring theme, with three tiers and lavender buttercream icing. The first and second layers were separated by strawberry jam and the second and third with honey. The decadent dessert was the tastiest thing I had ever eaten. By the end of the night, my feet were sore and my face ached from all the smiling.

Slowly, the guests filtered out as the evening came to an end. As the last of the guests left, I collapsed onto a bench next to Megan. She had kicked off her shoes and was rubbing the soles of her feet. She had danced through almost every song that evening. After spending her entire life looking in from the outside, she finally had friends and could let loose.

I smiled at her. "Thanks for being here today."

"I wouldn't—" Megan stopped as a shadow loomed over us.

I turned my head. My lips pressed into a straight line as an unexpected guest came into view. While Miranda hadn't been hostile since she'd been relocated here by the Warden Home Office, she hadn't exactly been friendly either. She was a cool cucumber on the best of days and someone who outright ignored me on the worst.

Why is she here? I plastered on a friendly smile and stood. "Miranda, I didn't expect to see you today."

She clasped her hands in front of her, her black robes billowing behind her as she came to a stop in front of us. "Well, yes. I suppose congratulations are in order. May you find the happiness you deserve."

"Thank you?" I wasn't entirely sure if that was a good or bad wish. It could be taken either way.

"I didn't plan on being a party crasher, but I'm here on official business."

My mouth went dry. "What is it?"

Miranda smoothed her hands down her stomach as if

trying to settle it. "We have been experiencing some difficulties in coordinating efforts with the local government. The Council has decided that we need a liaison to help bridge the gap between the Wardens and the city council."

I groaned. "I just got married, I—"

"I wasn't here for you." Miranda's eyes turned from my face to Megan's. "You start on Monday."

"What? I—You're kidding, right? I have a farm to take care of." Megan floundered.

"I'll see you at our offices downtown at eight a.m. sharp." Miranda turned on her heel. "Don't be late."

Megan and I stared after her, our mouths gaping.

What was that? I turned to Megan, grabbing her hand. "Wow. That's... you'll do great. If you want it."

"Do you think so?" Megan asked.

I nodded. "You're hardworking. You're one of the nicest people I know. They would be idiots not to love working with you."

"Thanks." Megan smiled. "I should head out. I've got a new job to prepare for. Good night, Dani. You were a beautiful bride."

I pulled her into a hug before she could walk away. She squeezed me back then strode toward the parking lot. I watched her leave. A liaison job would not be easy, but now that her curse was broken, people tended to like her. I could understand why she'd been chosen. She really would be great.

Chris came up behind me and wrapped his arms around my waist. "You ready to head home?"

My heart fluttered at the word "home." Since we'd gotten engaged, we had bounced back and forth between Chris's house and mine. This morning, his townhome had gone on the market, and he was officially moving in. I leaned into him and smiled up at the sky. "Definitely."

Chris drove us home. We held hands the whole way. He

parked in the driveway, and we walked up to the front door. I unlocked it and pushed open the door. I had just moved to take the first step inside when Chris stopped me with a hand on my shoulder. He spun me around and picked me up. My squeal turned into a laugh as he strode forward through the front door, carrying me bridal style.

Standing in the living room, with his arms still under my legs and waist, he kissed me gently. "Welcome home, Mrs. Harris."

Curious to see what happens with Megan Miller as the liaison to the Wardens of the West? You can get the first book in her series, 'Murder Among the Hives,' here.

In Book 1, Megan Miller's first day as a magical liaison comes with one small complication—murder.

After a lifetime of homesteading on Whidbey Island with her familiar, a stubborn dairy cow named Gertie, Megan's ready for a new challenge. When she volunteers to triage who should be investigating a suspicious death, the Sheriff or the Wardens, she figures she might brush up against something supernatural—but she doesn't expect the case to hit quite so close to home.

The victim was a local beekeeper—and ever since her death, the hives have turned unusually aggressive. As Megan digs deeper, she uncovers tangled secrets where magical motives and mundane grudges blur. If she can't solve the case, her new job will be over before it's even begun.

Perfect for fans of witchy small towns, magical mysteries, and charming animal sidekicks, this paranormal cozy will have you spellbound.

ALSO BY ELOISE EVERHART

A Williams Witch Mystery

Potions and the Pleasantly Poisoned

Tomes and the Tangled Trail

Divinations and the Disappearing Dead

Hexes and the Haunted House

Spells and the Suspiciously Silent

Grimoires and the Ghostly Guest

Enchantments and the Eerily Ensnared

Rituals and the Restless Remains

Charms and the Cursed Coven

A Miller's Magical Mystery

Murder Among the Hives

Murder Between the Stacks

JOIN MY NEWSLETTER

Interested in receiving bonus content like inspiration character art? If so, join our mailing list and receive access to fun things like 'Foresight and the Fateful Ferry,' and character cards. Go on an adventure with Dani and Chris as they journey into Seattle for a fun day out, and things take a dramatic turn when they stumble upon a dead body on the ferry.

ABOUT THE AUTHOR

Eloise Everhart lives in the Pacific Northwest. Her childhood was marked by voracious reading and tabletop roleplaying games, fueling her lifelong passion for storytelling.

By day, she's a dedicated insurance adjuster. It's a career that has honed her sharp eye for detail and developed her inquisitive mind—a skillset she now seamlessly integrates into her cozy mystery writing.

Beyond her storytelling ardor, Eloise is a devoted wife, sharing her home with a menagerie of rescued cats and dogs who have found their furever home in the Everhart household.

ACKNOWLEDGMENTS

I am forever thankful for my editors, Rashida Breen and Amanda Kruse. Rashida, you helped make the final book in this series hit all the important emotional points, and the big reveals feel even bigger. And Amanda, you really made the sentences flow.

To my husband, Nate, you have once again been my rock as I worked into the wee hours of the morning finishing this book. I really would not have been able to do complete this series without your endless support.

To my sister, Andrea, and my parents, you fostered my creative confidence early and often. You let me believe that my dreams of becoming an author were worthwhile. I will forever be thankful for that.

And to my best friend, Andrew, who is no longer with us. I will carry you with me, always. I think you would have really enjoyed this series.

"Come on a journey with me."

www.ingramcontent.com/pod-product-compliance
Lightning Source LLC
La Vergne TN
LVHW091147080826
845145LV00008B/2281

* 9 7 8 1 9 6 2 7 5 9 0 8 3 *